HORRID HENRY'S
CRACKING
CHRISTMAS

Francesca Simon spent her childhood in
California, and then went to Yale and Oxford
Universities to study medieval history and
literature. She now lives in London with her
family. She has written over fifty books and
won the Children's Book Of The Year in
2008 at the Galaxy British Book Awards for
Horrid Henry And The Abominable Snowman.

Tony Ross is of one Britain's best known
illustrators, with many picture books to his name.
He has also produced the line drawings for many
fiction titles, for authors such as David Walliams,
Jeanne Willis, Enid Blyton, Astrid Lindgren,
and many more. He lives in Wales.

Also by Francesca Simon

Don't Cook Cinderella
Helping Hercules

and for younger readers

Don't Be Horrid, Henry
The Parent Swap Shop
Spider School
The Topsy-Turvies

For a complete list of *Horrid Henry* titles
see the end of the book, or visit
www.horridhenry.co.uk
or
www.orionchildrensbooks.com

HORRID HENRY'S
CRACKING
CHRISTMAS

Francesca Simon

Illustrated by Tony Ross

Orion
Children's Books

This collection first published in Great Britain in 2015
by Orion Children's Books
an imprint of Hachette Children's Group
a division of Hodder and Stoughton Ltd
Carmelite House
50 Victoria Embankment
London EC4Y 0DZ

An Hachette UK Company

3 5 7 9 10 8 6 4

The paper and board used in this paperback are natural and
recyclable products made from wood grown in sustainable forests.
The manufacturing processes conform to the environmental
regulations of the country of origin.

A catalogue record for this book is available from the British Library.

Printed in Great Britain by Clays Ltd, St Ives plc

ISBN 978 1 5101 0048 0

www.horridhenry.co.uk
www.orionchildrensbooks.com

CONTENTS

CHECK OUT HENRY'S CHRISTMAS COUNTDOWN INSIDE

Horrid Henry's Christmas Play   13

Horrid Henry and the
Abominable Snowman   43

Horrid Henry's Christmas Presents   75

Horrid Henry's Ambush   99

Horrid Henry's Christmas   125

Horrid Henry's Christmas Lunch   153

How to Survive Christmas
Chaos with Horrid Henry   183

DECEMBER 1ST

24
DAYS TILL
CHRISTMAS!

Why is it always cold at Christmas?

Because it's Decembrrrr!

DECEMBER 2ND

23
DAYS TILL CHRISTMAS!

What bird has wings but can't fly?

A roast turkey.

DECEMBER 3RD

22
DAYS TILL
CHRISTMAS!

What do you call a reindeer wearing ear muffs?

Anything you want because he can't hear you!

HORRID HENRY'S CHRISTMAS PLAY

Horrid Henry slumped on the carpet
and willed the clock to go faster. Only
five more minutes to hometime! Already
Henry could taste those crisps he'd be
sneaking from the cupboard.

Miss Battle-Axe droned on about
school dinners (yuck), the new
drinking fountain blah blah blah, maths
homework blah blah blah, the school
Christmas play blah blah . . . what? Did

13

Miss Battle-Axe say . . . Christmas play? Horrid Henry sat up.

'This is a brand-new play with singing and dancing,' continued Miss Battle-Axe. 'And both the older and the younger children are taking part this year.'

Singing! Dancing! Showing off in front of the whole school! Years ago, when Henry was in the infants' class, he'd played eighth sheep in the nativity play and had snatched the baby from the manger and refused to hand him back. Henry hoped Miss Battle-Axe wouldn't remember.

Because Henry had to play the lead. He had to. Who else but Henry could be an all-singing, all-dancing Joseph?

'I want to be Mary,' shouted every girl in the class.

'I want to be a wise man!' shouted Rude Ralph.

'I want to be a sheep!' shouted Anxious Andrew.

14

'I want to be Joseph!' shouted Horrid Henry.

'No, me!' shouted Jazzy Jim.

'Me!' shouted Brainy Brian.

'Quiet!' shrieked Miss Battle-Axe. 'I'm the director, and my decision about who will act which part is final. I've cast the play as follows: Margaret. You will be Mary.' She handed her a thick script.

Moody Margaret whooped with joy. All the other girls glared at her.

'Susan, front legs of the donkey; Linda, hind legs; cows, Fiona and Clare. Blades of grass—' Miss Battle-Axe continued assigning parts.

Pick me for Joseph, pick me for Joseph, Horrid Henry begged silently. Who better than the best actor in the school to play the starring part?

'I'm a sheep, I'm a sheep, I'm a

15

beautiful sheep!' warbled Singing Soraya.

'I'm a shepherd!' beamed Jolly Josh.

'I'm an angel,' trilled Magic Martha.

'I'm a blade of grass,' sobbed Weepy William.

'Joseph will be played by—'

'ME!' screamed Henry.

'Me!' screamed New Nick, Greedy Graham, Dizzy Dave and Aerobic Al.

'—Peter,' said Miss Battle-Axe. 'From Miss Lovely's class.'

Horrid Henry felt as if he'd been slugged in the stomach. Perfect Peter?

16

His *younger* brother? Perfect Peter get the starring part?

'It's not fair!' howled Horrid Henry.

Miss Battle-Axe glared at him.

'Henry, you're—' Miss Battle-Axe consulted her list. Please not a blade of grass, please not a blade of grass, prayed Horrid Henry, shrinking. That would be just like Miss Battle-Axe, to humiliate him. Anything but that—

'—the innkeeper.'

The innkeeper! Horrid Henry sat up, beaming. How stupid he'd been: the *innkeeper* must be the starring part. Henry could see himself now, polishing glasses, throwing darts, pouring out big foaming Fizzywizz drinks to all his happy customers while singing a song about the joys of innkeeping. Then he'd get into a nice long argument about why there was no room at the inn, and finally, the chance to slam the door in Moody

17

Margaret's face after he'd pushed her away. Wow. Maybe he'd even get a second song. 'Ten Green Bottles' would fit right into the story: he'd sing and dance while knocking his less talented classmates off a wall. Wouldn't that be fun!

Miss Battle-Axe handed a page to Henry. 'Your script,' she said.

Henry was puzzled. Surely there were some pages missing?

He read:

(Joseph knocks. The innkeeper opens the door.)

JOSEPH: Is there any room at the inn?
INNKEEPER: No.

(The innkeeper shuts the door.)

Horrid Henry turned over the page.
It was blank. He held it up to the
light.

There was no secret writing. That was it.

His entire part was one line. One stupid
puny line. Not even a line, a word. 'No.'

Where was his song? Where was his
dance with the bottles and the guests at
the inn? How could he, Horrid Henry,
the best actor in the class (and indeed,
the world) be given just one word in the
school play? Even the donkeys got a song.

Worse, after he said his *one* word,
Perfect Peter and Moody Margaret got to
yack for hours about mangers and wise
men and shepherds and sheep, and then

sing a duet, while he, Henry, hung about behind the hay with the blades of grass.

It was so unfair!

He should be the star of the show, not his stupid worm of a brother. Why on earth was Peter cast as Joseph anyway? He was a terrible actor. He couldn't sing, he just squeaked like a squished toad. And why was Margaret playing Mary? Now she'd never stop bragging and swaggering.

AAAARRRRGGGGHHHH!

'Isn't it exciting!' said Mum.

'Isn't it thrilling!' said Dad. 'Our little boy, the star of the show.'

'Well done, Peter,' said Mum.

'We're so proud of you,' said Dad.

Perfect Peter smiled modestly.

'Of course I'm not *really* the star,' he said, 'Everyone's important, even little parts like the blades of grass and the innkeeper.'

Horrid Henry pounced. He was a Great White shark lunging for the kill.

'AAAARRRRGGGHH!' squealed Peter. 'Henry bit me!'

'Henry! Don't be horrid!' snapped Mum.

'Henry! Go to your room!' snapped Dad.

Horrid Henry stomped upstairs and slammed the door. How could he bear

21

the humiliation of playing the innkeeper when Peter was the star? He'd just have to force Peter to switch roles with him. Henry was sure he could find a way to persuade Peter, but persuading Miss Battle-Axe was a different matter. Miss Battle-Axe had a mean, horrible way of never doing what Henry wanted.

Maybe he could trick Peter into leaving the show. Yes! And then nobly offer to replace him.

But unfortunately, there was no guarantee Miss Battle-Axe would give Henry Peter's role. She'd probably just replace Peter with Goody-Goody Gordon. He was stuck.

And then Horrid Henry had a brilliant, spectacular idea. Why hadn't he thought of this before? If he couldn't play a bigger part, he'd just have to make his part bigger. For instance, he could *scream* 'No.' *That* would get a reaction. Or he could bellow

'No,' and then hit Joseph. I'm an angry
innkeeper, thought Horrid Henry, and I
hate guests coming to my inn. Certainly
smelly ones like Joseph. Or he could
shout 'No!', hit Joseph, then rob him.
I'm a robber innkeeper, thought Henry.
Or, I'm a robber *pretending* to be an innkeeper. That would liven up the play a
bit. Maybe he could be a French robber
innkeeper, shout '*Non*', and rob Mary
and Joseph. Or he was a French robber
pirate innkeeper, so he could shout '*Non*,'
tie Mary and Joseph up and make them
walk the plank.

Hmmm,
thought
Horrid
Henry.
Maybe
my
part
won't be

so small. After all, the innkeeper *was* the most important character.

Rehearsals had been going on forever. Horrid Henry spent most of his time slumping in a chair. He'd never seen such a boring play. Naturally he'd done everything he could to improve it.

'Can't I add a dance?' asked Henry.

'No,' snapped Miss Battle-Axe.

'Can't I add a teeny-weeny-little song?'
Henry pleaded.

'No!' said Miss
Battle-Axe.

'But how does the
innkeeper *know* there's
no room?' said Henry.
'I think I should—'

Miss Battle-Axe
glared at him with
her red eyes.

'One more word from you, Henry, and you'll change places with Linda,' snapped Miss Battle-Axe. 'Blades of grass, let's try again . . .'

Eeek! An innkeeper with one word was infinitely better than being invisible as the hind legs of a donkey. Still—it was so unfair. He was only trying to help.

Showtime! Not a teatowel was to be found in any local shop. Mums and dads had been up all night frantically sewing costumes. Now the waiting and the rehearsing were over.

Everyone lined up on stage behind the curtain. Peter and Margaret waited on the side to make their big entrance as Mary and Joseph.

'Isn't it exciting, Henry, being in a real play?' whispered Peter.

'NO,' snarled Henry.

'Places, everyone, for the opening song,' hissed Miss Battle-Axe. 'Now remember, don't worry if you make a little mistake: just carry on and no one will notice.'

'But I still think I should have an argument with Mary and Joseph about whether there's room,' said Henry. 'Shouldn't I at least check to see—'

'No!' snapped Miss Battle-Axe, glaring at him. 'If I hear another peep from you, Henry, you will sit behind the bales of hay and Jim will play your part. Blades of grass! Line up with the donkeys! Sheep! Get ready to baaa . . . Bert! Are you a sheep or a blade of grass?'

'I dunno,' said Beefy Bert.

Mrs Oddbod went to the front of the stage. 'Welcome everyone, mums and dads, boys and girls, to our new Christmas play, a little different from previous years. We hope you all enjoy a brand new show!'

Miss Battle-Axe started the CD player. The music pealed. The curtain rose. The audience stamped and cheered. Stars twinkled. Cows mooed. Horses neighed. Sheep baa'ed. Cameras flashed.

Horrid Henry stood in the wings and watched the shepherds do their Highland dance. He still hadn't decided for sure how he was going to play his part. There were so many possibilities. It was so hard to choose.

Finally, Henry's big moment arrived.

He strode across the stage and waited behind the closed inn door for Mary and Joseph.

Knock!

Knock!

Knock!

The innkeeper stepped forward and opened the door. There was Moody Margaret, simpering away as Mary, and Perfect Peter looking full of himself as Joseph.

'Is there any room at the inn?' asked Joseph.

Good question, thought Horrid Henry. His mind was blank. He'd thought of so many great things he *could* say that what he was *supposed* to say had just gone straight out of his head.

'Is there any room at the inn?' repeated Joseph loudly.

'Yes,' said the innkeeper. 'Come on in.'

Joseph looked at Mary.

Mary looked at Joseph.

29

The audience murmured.

Oops, thought Horrid Henry. Now he remembered. He'd been supposed to say no. Oh well, in for a penny, in for a pound.

The innkeeper grabbed Mary and Joseph's sleeves and yanked them through the door. 'Come on in, I haven't got all day.'

' . . . but . . . but . . . the inn's *full*,' said Mary.

'No it isn't,' said the innkeeper.

'Is too.'

'Is not. It's my inn and I should know. This is the best inn in Bethlehem, we've got TVs and beds, and—' the innkeeper paused for a moment. What *did* inns have in them? '—and computers!'

Mary glared at the innkeeper.

The innkeeper glared at Mary.

Miss Battle-Axe gestured frantically from the wings.

'This inn looks full to me,' said Mary firmly. 'Come on Joseph, let's go to the stable.'

'Oh, don't go there, you'll get fleas,' said the innkeeper.

'So?' said Mary.

'I love fleas,' said Joseph weakly.

'And it's full of manure.'

'So are you,' snapped Mary.

'Don't be horrid, Mary,' said the innkeeper severely. 'Now sit down and

31

rest your weary bones and I'll sing you a song.' And the innkeeper started singing:

'Ten green bottles, standing on a wall
Ten green bottles, standing on a wall,
And if one green bottle should accidentally
*   fall—'*

'OOOHHH!' moaned Mary. 'I'm having the baby.'

'Can't you wait till I've finished my song?' snapped the inkeeper.

'NO!' bellowed Mary.

Miss Battle-Axe drew her hand across her throat.

Henry ignored her. After all, the show must go on.

'Come on, Joseph,' interrupted Mary. 'We're going to the stable.'

'OK,' said Joseph.

'You're making a big mistake,' said the innkeeper. 'We've got satellite TV and . . . '

Miss Battle-Axe ran on stage and
nabbed him.

'Thank you, innkeeper, your other
guests need you now,' said Miss Battle-
Axe, grabbing him by the collar.

'Merry Christmas!' shrieked Horrid
Henry as she yanked him off-stage.

There was a very long silence.

'Bravo!' yelled Moody Margaret's deaf
aunt.

Mum and Dad weren't sure what to
do. Should they clap, or run away to a
place where no one knew them?

Mum clapped.

Dad hid his face in his hands.

'Do you think anyone noticed?' whispered Mum.

Dad looked at Mrs Oddbod's grim face. He sank down in his chair. Maybe one day he would learn how to make himself invisible.

'But what was I *supposed* to do?' said Horrid Henry afterwards in Mrs Oddbod's office. 'It's not *my* fault I forgot my line. Miss Battle-Axe said not to worry if we made a mistake and just to carry on.'

Could he help it if a star was born?

DECEMBER 4TH

21
DAYS TILL
CHRISTMAS!

(3 WEEKS TO GO!)

What kind of bread do elves use to make sandwiches?

Shortbread

DECEMBER 5TH

20

DAYS TILL CHRISTMAS!

What do snowmen sing at parties?

Freeze a jolly good fellow!

DECEMBER 6TH

19

DAYS TILL
CHRISTMAS!

What happened to the thief who stole a Christmas calendar?

He got 12 months!

HORRID HENRY
AND THE ABOMINABLE SNOWMAN

Moody Margaret took aim.

Thwack!

A snowball whizzed past and smacked Sour Susan in the face.

'AAAAARRGGHHH!' shrieked Susan.

'Ha ha, got you,' said Margaret.

'You big meanie,' howled Susan, scooping up a fistful of snow and hurling it at Margaret.

Thwack!

Susan's snowball smacked Moody Margaret in the face.

'OWWWW!' screamed Margaret.
'You've blinded me.'

'Good!' screamed Susan.

'I hate you!' shouted Margaret, shoving
Susan.

'I hate you more!' shouted Susan,
pushing Margaret.

Splat! Margaret toppled into the snow.

Splat! Susan toppled into the snow.

'I'm going home to build my own
snowman,' sobbed Susan.

'Fine. I'll win without you,' said
Margaret.

'Won't!'

'Will! I'm going to win, copycat,'
shrieked Margaret.

'*I'm* going to win,' shrieked Susan. 'I
kept my best ideas secret.'

'Win? Win what?' demanded Horrid
Henry, stomping down his front steps in
his snow boots and swaggering over. Henry
could hear the word *win* from miles away.

'Haven't you heard about the competition?' said Sour Susan. 'The prize is—'

'Shut up! Don't tell him,' shouted Moody Margaret, packing snow onto her snowman's head.

Win? Competition? Prize? Horrid Henry's ears quivered. What secret were they trying to keep from him? Well, not for long. Horrid Henry was an expert at extracting information.

45

'Oh, the competition. I know all about *that*,' lied Horrid Henry. 'Hey, great snowman,' he added, strolling casually over to Margaret's snowman and pretending to admire her work.

Now, what should he do? Torture? Margaret's ponytail was always a tempting target. And snow down her jumper would make her talk.

What about blackmail? He could spread some great rumours about Margaret at school. Or . . .

'Tell me about the competition or the ice guy gets it,' said Horrid Henry suddenly, leaping over to the snowman and putting his hands round its neck.

'You wouldn't dare,' gasped Moody Margaret.

Henry's mittened hands got ready to push.

'Bye bye, head,' hissed Horrid Henry. 'Nice knowing you.'

Margaret's snowman wobbled.

'Stop!' screamed Margaret. 'I'll tell you. It doesn't matter 'cause you'll never ever win.'

'Keep talking,' said Horrid Henry warily, watching out in case Susan tried to ambush him from behind.

'Frosty Freeze are having a best snowman competition,' said Moody Margaret, glaring. 'The winner gets a year's free supply of ice cream. The judges will decide tomorrow morning.

Now get away from my snowman.'

Horrid Henry walked off in a daze, his jaw dropping. Margaret and Susan pelted him with snowballs but Henry didn't even notice. Free ice cream for a year direct from the Frosty Freeze Ice Cream factory. Oh wow! Horrid Henry couldn't believe it. Mum and Dad were so mean and horrible they hardly ever let him have ice cream. And when they did, they never *ever* let him put on his own hot fudge sauce and whipped cream and sprinkles. Or even scoop the ice cream himself. Oh no.

Well, when he won the Best Snowman Competition they couldn't stop him gorging on Chunky Chocolate Fab Fudge Caramel Delight, or Vanilla Whip Tutti-Fruitti Toffee Treat. Oh boy! Henry could taste that glorious ice cream now. He'd live on ice cream. He'd bathe in ice cream. He'd sleep in ice cream. Everyone from school would turn up at his house when the Frosty Freeze truck arrived bringing his weekly barrels. No matter how much they begged, Horrid Henry would send them all away. No way was he sharing a drop of his precious ice cream with *anyone*.

And all he had to do was to build the best snowman in the neighbourhood. Pah! Henry's was sure to be the winner. He would build the biggest snowman of all. And not just a snowman. A snowman with claws, and horns, and fangs. A vampire-demon-monster snowman. An Abominable Snowman. Yes!

Henry watched Margaret and
Susan rolling snow and packing their
saggy snowman. Ha. Snow heap, more
like.

'You'll never win with *that*,' jeered
Horrid Henry. 'Your snowman is
pathetic.'

'Better than yours,' snapped Margaret.
Horrid Henry rolled his eyes.

'Obviously, because I haven't started mine yet.'

'We've got a big head start on you, so ha ha ha,' said Susan. 'We're building a ballerina snowgirl.'

'Shut up, Susan,' screamed Margaret.

A ballerina snowgirl? What a stupid idea. If that was the best they could do Henry was sure to win.

'Mine will be the biggest, the best, the most gigantic snowman ever seen,' said Horrid Henry. 'And much better than your stupid snow dwarf.'

'Fat chance,' sneered Margaret.

'Yeah, Henry,' sneered Susan. 'Ours is the best.'

'No way,' said Horrid Henry, starting to roll a gigantic ball of snow for Abominable's big belly. There was no time to lose.

Roll.

Roll.

Roll.

Up the path, down the path, across the garden, down the side, back and forth, back and forth, Horrid Henry rolled the biggest ball of snow ever seen.

'Henry, can I build a snowman with you?' came a little voice.

'No,' said Henry, starting to carve out some clawed feet.

'Oh please,' said Peter. 'We could build a great big one together. Like a bunny snowman, or a—'

'No!' said Henry. 'It's *my* snowman. Build your own.'

'Muuuummmm!' wailed Peter. 'Henry won't let me build a snowman with him.'

'Don't be horrid, Henry,' said Mum. 'Why don't you build one together?'

'NO!!!' said Horrid Henry. He wanted to make his *own* snowman.

If he built a snowman with his stupid worm brother, he'd have to share the prize. Well, no way. He wanted all

that ice cream for himself. And his
Abominable Snowman was sure to be the
best. Why share a prize when you didn't
have to?

'Get away from my snowman, Peter,'
hissed Henry.

Perfect Peter snivelled. Then he started
to roll a tiny ball of snow.

'And get your own snow,' said Henry.
'All this is mine.'

'Muuuuuum!' wailed Peter. 'Henry's
hogging all the snow.'

★

'We're done,' trilled Moody Margaret.
'Beat *this* if you can.'

Horrid Henry looked at Margaret and
Susan's snowgirl, complete with a big
pink tutu wound round the waist. It was
as big as Margaret.

'That old heap of snow is nothing compared to *mine*,' bragged Horrid Henry.

Moody Margaret and Sour Susan looked at Henry's Abominable Snowman, complete with Viking horned helmet, fangs, and hairy scary claws. It was a few centimetres taller than Henry.

'Nah nah ne nah nah, mine's bigger,' boasted Henry.

'Nah nah ne nah nah, mine's better,' boasted Margaret.

'How do you like *my* snowman?' said Peter. 'Do you think *I* could win?'

Horrid Henry stared at Perfect Peter's tiny snowman. It didn't even have a head, just a long, thin, lumpy body with two stones stuck in the top for eyes.

Horrid Henry howled with laughter.

'That's the worst snowman I've ever seen,' said Henry. 'It doesn't even have a head. That's a snow carrot.'

'It is not,' wailed Peter. 'It's a big bunny.'

'Henry! Peter! Suppertime,' called Mum.

Henry stuck out his tongue at Margaret.

'And don't you dare touch my snowman.'

Margaret stuck out her tongue at Henry.

'And don't you dare touch *my* snowgirl.'

'I'll be watching you, Margaret.'

'I'll be watching *you*, Henry.'

They glared at each other.

Henry woke.

What was that noise? Was Margaret sabotaging his snowman? Was Susan stealing his snow?

Horrid Henry dashed to the window.

Phew. There was his Abominable Snowman, big as ever, dwarfing every other snowman in the street. Henry's was definitely the biggest, and the best. Umm boy, he could taste that Triple Fudge Gooey Chocolate Chip Peanut Butter Marshmallow Custard ice cream right now.

Horrid Henry climbed back into bed.

A tiny doubt nagged him.

Was his snowman *definitely* bigger than Margaret's?

'Course it was, thought Henry.

'Are you sure?' rumbled his tummy.

'Yeah,' said Henry.

'Because I really want that ice cream,' growled his tummy. 'Why don't you double-check?'

Horrid Henry got out of bed.

He was sure his was bigger and better than Margaret's. He was absolutely sure his was bigger and better.

But what if—

I can't sleep without checking, thought Henry.

Tip toe.

Tip toe.

Tip toe.

Horrid Henry slipped out of the front door.

The whole street was silent and white and frosty. Every house had a snowman in front. All of them much smaller than Henry's, he noted with satisfaction.

And there was his Abominable Snowman looming up, Viking horns scraping the sky. Horrid Henry gazed at him proudly. Next to him was Peter's pathetic pimple, with its stupid black stones. A snow lump, thought Henry.

Then he looked over at Margaret's snowgirl. Maybe it had fallen down, thought Henry hopefully. And if it hadn't maybe he could help it on its way . . .

He looked again. And again. That evil fiend!

Margaret had sneaked an extra ball of snow on top, complete with a huge flowery hat.

That little cheater, thought Horrid
Henry indignantly. She'd sneaked out
after bedtime and made hers bigger
than his. How dare she? Well, he'd fix
Margaret. He'd add more snow to his
right away.

Horrid Henry looked around. Where could he find more snow? He'd already used up every drop on his front lawn to build his giant, and no new snow had fallen.

Henry shivered.

Brr, it was freezing. He needed more snow, and he needed it fast. His slippers were starting to feel very wet and cold.

Horrid Henry eyed Peter's pathetic lump of snow. Hmmn, thought Horrid Henry.

Hmmn, thought Horrid Henry again.

Well, it's not doing any good sitting

there, thought Henry. Someone could trip over it. Someone could hurt themselves. In fact, Peter's snowlump was a danger. He had to act fast before someone fell over it and broke a leg.

Quickly, he scooped up Peter's

snowman and stacked it carefully on top of his. Then standing on his tippy toes, he balanced the Abominable Snowman's Viking horns on top.

Da dum!

Much better. And *much* bigger than Margaret's.

Teeth chattering, Horrid Henry sneaked back into his house and crept into bed. Ice cream, here I come, thought Horrid Henry.

Ding dong.

Horrid Henry jumped out of bed. What a morning to oversleep.

Perfect Peter ran and opened the door.

'We're from the Frosty Freeze Ice Cream Factory,' said the man, beaming. 'And you've got the winning snowman out front.'

'I won!' screeched Horrid Henry. 'I won!' He tore down the stairs and out

the door. Oh what a lovely lovely day.
The sky was blue. The sun was shining
— huh???

Horrid Henry looked around.

Horrid Henry's Abominable Snowman
was gone.

'Margaret!' screamed Henry. 'I'll kill
you!'

But Moody Margaret's snowgirl was
gone, too.

The Abominable Snowman's helmet
lay on its side on the ground. All that was
left of Henry's snowman was . . . Peter's
pimple, with its two black stone eyes. A
big blue ribbon was pinned to the top.

'But that's *my* snowman,' said Perfect Peter.

'But . . . but . . .' said Horrid Henry.

'You mean, *I* won?' said Peter.

'That's wonderful, Peter,' said Mum.

'That's fantastic, Peter,' said Dad.

'All the others melted,' said the Frosty Freeze man. 'Yours was the only one left. It must have been a giant.'

'It was,' howled Horrid Henry.

DECEMBER 7ᵀᴴ

18
DAYS TILL
CHRISTMAS!

What kind of
ball doesn't bounce?

A snowball.

DECEMBER 8TH

17
DAYS TILL
CHRISTMAS!

How do you get milk from a reindeer?

Rob its fridge and run like mad.

DECEMBER 9TH

16
DAYS TILL
CHRISTMAS!

How does good King Wenceslas like his pizzas?

Deep pan, crisp and even.

HORRID HENRY'S
CHRISTMAS
PRESENTS

Horrid Henry sat by the Christmas tree
and stuffed himself full of the special
sweets he'd nicked from the special
Christmas Day stash when Mum and Dad
weren't looking. After his triumph in the
school Christmas play, Horrid Henry was
feeling delighted with himself and with
the world.

Granny and Grandpa, his grown-up
cousins Pimply Paul and Prissy Polly, and

their baby Vomiting Vera were coming
to spend Christmas. Whoopee, thought
Horrid Henry, because they'd all have
to bring *him* presents. Thankfully, Rich
Aunt Ruby and Stuck-Up Steve weren't
coming. They were off skiing. Henry
hadn't forgotten the dreadful lime green
cardigan Aunt Ruby had given him last
year. And much as he hated cousin Polly,
anyone was better than Stuck-Up Steve,
even someone who squealed all the
time and had a baby who threw up on
everyone.

Mum dashed into the sitting room,
wearing a flour-covered apron and
looking frantic. Henry choked down
his mouthful of sweets.

'Right, who wants to decorate
the tree?' said Mum. She held out a
cardboard box brimming with tinsel and
gold and silver and blue baubles.

'Me!' said Henry.

'Me!' said Peter.

Horrid Henry dashed to the box and scooped up as many shiny ornaments as he could.

'I want to put on the gold baubles,' said Henry.

'I want to put on the tinsel,' said Peter.

'Keep away from my side of the tree,' hissed Henry.

'You don't have a side,' said Peter.

'Do too.'

'Do not,' said Peter.

'I want to put on the tinsel *and* the baubles,' said Henry.

77

'But I want to do the tinsel,' said Peter.

'Tough,' said Henry, draping Peter in tinsel.

'Muuum!' wailed Peter. 'Henry's hogging all the decorations! And he's putting tinsel on me.'

'Don't be horrid, Henry,' said Mum. 'Share with your brother.'

Peter carefully wrapped blue tinsel round the lower branches.

'Don't put it there,' said Henry, yanking it off. Trust Peter to ruin his beautiful plan.

'MUUUM!' wailed Peter.

'He's wrecking my design,' screeched Henry. 'He doesn't know how to decorate a tree.'

'But I wanted it there!' protested Peter. 'Leave my tinsel alone.'

'You leave my stuff alone then,' said Henry.

'He's wrecked my design!' shrieked

Henry and Peter.

'Stop fighting, both of you!' shrieked Mum.

'He started it!' screamed Henry.

'Did not!'

'Did too!'

'That's enough,' said Mum. 'Now, whose turn is it to put the fairy on top?'

'I don't want to have that stupid fairy,' wailed Horrid Henry. 'I want to have Terminator Gladiator instead.'

'No,' said Peter. 'I want the fairy. We've always had the fairy.'

'Terminator!'

'Fairy!'

'TERMINATOR!'

'FAIRY!'

Slap Slap

'WAAAAAAA!'

'We're having the fairy,' said Mum firmly, 'and *I'll* put it on the tree.'

'NOOOOOO!' screamed Henry. 'Why can't we do what I want to do? I never get to have what I want.'

'Liar!' whimpered Peter.

'I've had enough of this,' said Mum. 'Now get your presents and put them under the tree.'

Peter ran off.

Henry stood still.

'Henry,' said Mum. 'Have you finished wrapping your Christmas presents?'

Yikes, thought Horrid Henry. What am I going to do now? The moment he'd been dreading for weeks had arrived.

'Henry! I'm not going to ask you again,' said Mum. 'Have you finished wrapping all your Christmas presents?'

'Yes!' bellowed Horrid Henry.

This was not entirely true. Henry had not finished wrapping his Christmas presents. In fact, he hadn't even started. The truth was, Henry had finished wrapping because he had no presents to wrap.

This was certainly *not* his fault. He *had* bought a few gifts, certainly. He knew Peter would love the box of green Day-Glo slime. And if he didn't, well, he knew who to give it to. And Granny and Grandpa and Mum and Dad and Paul and Polly would have adored the big boxes of chocolates Henry had won at the school fair. Could he help it if the chocolates had called his name so loudly that he'd been forced to eat them all? And then Granny had been complaining about gaining weight. Surely it would have been very unkind to give her chocolate. And eating chocolate would have just made Pimply Paul's pimples worse. Henry'd done him a big favour eating that box.

And it was hardly Henry's fault when he'd needed extra goo for a raid on the Secret Club and Peter's present was the only stuff to hand? He'd *meant* to buy replacements. But he had so many things he needed to buy for himself that when he opened his skeleton bank to get out some cash for Christmas shopping, only 35p had rolled out.

'I've bought and wrapped all *my* presents, Mum,' said Perfect Peter. 'I've been saving my pocket money for months.'

'Whoopee for you,' said Henry.

'Henry, it's always better to give than
to receive,' said Peter.

Mum beamed. 'Quite right, Peter.'

'Says who?' growled Horrid Henry. 'I'd
much rather *get* presents.'

'Don't be so horrid, Henry,' said Mum.

'Don't be so selfish, Henry,' said Dad.

Horrid Henry stuck out his tongue.

Mum and Dad gasped.

'You horrid boy,' said Mum.

'I just hope Father Christmas didn't see
that,' said Dad.

'Henry,' said Peter, 'Father Christmas

won't bring you any presents if you're bad.'

AAARRRGGHHH! Horrid Henry sprang at Peter. He was a grizzly bear guzzling a juicy morsel.

'AAAAIIEEE,' wailed Peter. 'Henry pinched me.'

'Henry! Go to your room,' said Mum.

'Fine!' screamed Horrid Henry, stomping off and slamming the door. Why did he get stuck with the world's meanest and most horrible parents? *They* certainly didn't deserve any presents.

Presents! Why couldn't he just *get* them? Why oh why did he have to *give* them? Giving other people presents was such a waste of his hard-earned money. Every time he gave a present it meant something he couldn't buy for himself. Goodbye chocolate. Goodbye comics. Goodbye Deluxe Goo-Shooter. And then, if you bought anything good, it was so horrible having to give it away. He'd practically cried having to give Ralph that Terminator Gladiator poster for his birthday. And the Mutant Max lunchbox Mum made him give Kasim still made him gnash his teeth whenever he saw Kasim with it.

Now he was stuck, on Christmas Eve, with no money, and no presents to give anyone, deserving or not.

And then Henry had a wonderful, spectacular idea. It was so wonderful, and so spectacular, that he couldn't

believe he hadn't thought of it before.
Who said he had to *buy* presents? Didn't
Mum and Dad always say it was the
thought that counted? And oh boy was
he thinking.

Granny was sure to love a Mutant
Max comic. After all, who wouldn't?
Then when she'd finished enjoying it,
he could borrow it back. Horrid Henry
rummaged under his bed and found a
recent copy. In fact, it would be a shame
if Grandpa got jealous of Granny's great
present. Safer to give them each one,
thought Henry, digging deep into his
pile to find one with the fewest torn
pages.

Now let's see, Mum and Dad. He
could draw them a lovely picture. Nah,
that would take too long. Even better,
he could write them a poem.

Henry sat down at his desk, grabbed
a pencil, and wrote:

Dear Old baldy Dad
Don't be sad
Be glad
Because you've had...
A very merry Christmas
Love from your lad,
Henry

Not bad, thought Henry. Not bad. And so cheap! Now one for Mum.

Dear old wrinkly Mum
Don't be glum
Cause you've got a fat tum
And an even bigger bum
Ho ho ho hum
Love from your son,

Henry

Wow! It was hard finding so many
words to rhyme with *mum* but he'd
done it. And the poem was nice and
Christmasy with the 'ho ho ho'. *Son*
didn't rhyme but hopefully Mum

wouldn't notice because she'd be so
thrilled with the rest of the poem.
When he was famous she'd be proud to
show off the poem her son had written
specially for her.

Now, Polly. Hmmmn.
She was always squeaking
and squealing about dirt
and dust. Maybe a lovely
kitchen sponge? Or a rag
she could use to mop up
after Vera? Or a bucket
to put over Pimply Paul's
head?

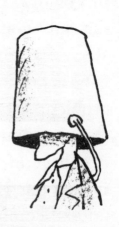

Wait. What about some soap?

Horrid Henry nipped into the
bathroom. Yes! There was a tempting
bar of blue soap going to waste in the
soap dish by the bathtub. True, it had
been used once or twice, but a bit of
smoothing with his fingers would sort
that out. In fact, Polly and Paul could

share this present, it was such a good one.

Whistling, Horrid Henry wrapped up the soap in sparkling reindeer paper. He was a genius. Why hadn't he ever done this before? And a lovely rag from under the sink would be perfect as a gag for Vera.

That just left Peter and all his present problems would be over. A piece of chewing gum, only one careful owner? A collage of sweet wrappers which spelled out *Worm*? The unused comb Peter had given *him* last Christmas?

Aha. Peter loved bunnies. What better present than a picture of a bunny?

It was the work of a few moments for Henry to draw a bunny

and slash a few blue lines across it to colour it in. Then he signed his name in big letters at the bottom. Maybe he should be a famous artist and not a poet when he grew up, he thought, admiring his handiwork. Henry had heard that artists got paid loads of cash just for stacking a few bricks or hurling paint at a white canvas. Being an artist sounded like a great job, since it left so much time for playing computer games.

Horrid Henry dumped his presents beneath the Christmas tree and sighed happily. This was one Christmas where he was sure to get a lot more than he gave. Whoopee! Who could ask for anything more?

DECEMBER 10ᵀᴴ

15

DAYS TILL
CHRISTMAS!

What is green, covered in tinsel and goes ribbet ribbet?

Mistle-toad!

DECEMBER 11ᵀᴴ

14
DAYS TILL
CHRISTMAS!

(JUST 2 WEEKS TO GO

Knock, knock!
Who's there?
Wayne.
Wayne who?

"Wayne in a manger.
No crib for a bed."

DECEMBER 12ᵀᴴ

13

DAYS TILL
CHRISTMAS!

What's the best thing to give your parents at Christmas?

A list of everything you want.

HORRID HENRY'S AMBUSH

It was Christmas Eve at last. Every minute felt like an hour. Every hour felt like a year. How could Henry live until Christmas morning when he could get his hands on all his loot?

Mum and Dad were baking frantically in the kitchen.

Perfect Peter sat by the twinkling Christmas tree scratching out 'Silent Night' over and over again on his cello.

'Can't you play something else?' snapped Henry.

'No,' said Peter, sawing away. 'This is the only Christmas carol I know. You can move if you don't like it.'

'You move,' said Henry.

Peter ignored him.

'Siiiiiiiii—lent Niiiiight,' screeched the cello.

AAARRRGH.

Horrid Henry lay on the sofa with his fingers in his ears, double-checking his choices from the Toy Heaven catalogue. Big red 'X's' appeared on every page, to help you-know-who remember all the toys he absolutely had to have. Oh please, let everything he wanted leap from its pages and into Santa's sack. After all, what could be better than looking at a huge glittering stack of presents on Christmas morning, and knowing that they were all for you?

Oh please let this be the year when he finally got everything he wanted!

His letter to Father Christmas couldn't have been clearer.

Dear Father Christmas,

I want loads and loads and loads of cash, to make up for the puny amount you put in my stocking last year. And a Robomatic Supersonic Space Howler Deluxe plus attachments would be great, too. I have asked for this before, you know!!! And the Terminator Gladiator fighting kit. I need lots more Day-Glo slime and comics and a Mutant Max poster and the new Zapatron Hip-Hop Dinosaur. This is your last chance.

Henry

PS. Satsumas are NOT presents!!!!!
PPS. Peter asked me to tell you to give me all his presents as he doesn't want any.

How hard could it be for Father Christmas to get this right? He'd asked for the Space Howler last year, and it never arrived. Instead, Henry got . . . vests. And handkerchiefs. And books. And clothes. And a—bleuccccck—jigsaw puzzle and a skipping rope and a tiny supersoaker instead of the mega-sized one he'd specified. Yuck! Father Christmas obviously needed Henry's help.

Father Christmas is getting old and doddery, thought Henry. Maybe he hasn't got my letters. Maybe he's lost his reading glasses. Or—what a horrible thought— maybe he was delivering Henry's presents by mistake to some other Henry. Eeeek!

Some yucky, undeserving Henry was probably right now this minute playing with Henry's Terminator Gladiator sword, shield, axe, and trident. And enjoying his Intergalactic Samurai Gorillas. It was so unfair!

And then suddenly Henry had a brilliant, spectacular idea. Why had he never thought of this before? All his present problems would be over. Presents were far too important to leave to Father Christmas. Since he couldn't be trusted to bring the right gifts, Horrid Henry had no choice. He would have to ambush Father Christmas.

Yes!

He'd hold Father Christmas hostage with his Goo-Shooter, while he rummaged in his present sack for all the loot he was owed. Maybe Henry would keep the lot. Now *that* would be fair.

Let's see, thought Horrid Henry. Father

Christmas was bound to be a slippery character, so he'd need to booby-trap his bedroom. When you-know-who sneaked in to fill his stocking at the end of the bed, Henry could leap up and nab him. Father Christmas had a lot of explaining to do for all those years of stockings filled with satsumas and walnuts instead of chocolate and cold hard cash.

So, how best to capture him?

Henry considered.

A bucket of water above the door.

A skipping rope stretched tight across the entrance, guaranteed to trip up intruders.

A web of string criss-crossed from bedpost to door and threaded with bells to ensnare night-time visitors.

And let's not forget strategically scattered whoopee cushions.

His plan was foolproof.

Loot, here I come, thought Horrid
Henry.

Horrid Henry sat up in bed, his Goo-
Shooter aimed at the half-open door
where a bucket of water balanced.

All his traps were laid. No one was getting in without Henry knowing about it. Any minute now, he'd catch Father Christmas and make him pay up.

Henry waited. And waited. And waited. His eyes started to feel heavy and he closed them for a moment.

There was a rustling at Henry's door.

Oh my god, this was it! Henry lay down and pretended to be asleep.

Cr-eeeek.

Cr-eeeek.

Horrid Henry reached for his Goo-Shooter.

A huge shape loomed in the doorway.

Henry braced himself to attack.

'Doesn't he look sweet when he's asleep?' whispered the shape.

'What a little snugglechops,'

whispered another.

Sweet? Snugglechops?

Horrid Henry's fingers itched to let Mum and Dad have it with both barrels.

POW!

Splat!

Henry could see it now. Mum covered in green goo. Dad covered in green goo. Mum and Dad snatching the Goo-Shooter and wrecking all his plans and throwing out all his presents and banning him from TV for ever . . . hmmmn. His fingers felt a little less itchy.

Henry lowered his Goo-Shooter. The bucket of water wobbled above the door.

Yikes! What if Mum and Dad stepped into his Santa traps? All his hard work—ruined.

'I'm awake,' snarled Henry.

The shapes stepped back. The water stopped wobbling.

'Go to sleep!' hissed Mum.

'Go to sleep!' hissed Dad.

'What are you doing here?' demanded Henry.

'Checking on you,' said Mum. 'Now go to sleep or Father Christmas will never come.'

He'd better, thought Henry.

Horrid Henry woke with a jolt. AAARRGGH! He'd fallen asleep. How could he? Panting and gasping Henry switched on the light. Phew. His traps were intact. His stocking was empty. Father Christmas hadn't been yet.

Wow, was that lucky. That was incredibly lucky. Henry lay back, his heart pounding.

And then Horrid Henry had a terrible thought.

What if Father Christmas had decided to be spiteful and *avoid* Henry's bedroom this year? Or what if he'd played a sneaky trick on Henry and filled a stocking *downstairs* instead?

Nah. No way.

But wait. When Father Christmas came to Rude Ralph's house he always filled the stockings downstairs. Now Henry came to think of it, Moody Margaret always left her stocking downstairs too, hanging from the fireplace, not from the end of her bed, like Henry did.

Horrid Henry looked at the clock.

It was past midnight. Mum and Dad had forbidden him to go downstairs till morning, on pain of having all his presents taken away and no telly all day.

But this was an emergency. He'd creep downstairs, take a quick peek to make sure he hadn't missed Father Christmas, then be back in bed in a jiffy.

No one will ever know, thought Horrid Henry.

Henry tiptoed round the whoopee cushions, leaped over the criss-cross threads, stepped over the skipping rope and carefully squeezed through his door so as not to disturb the bucket of water. Then he crept downstairs.

Sneak
    Sneak
        Sneak

Horrid Henry shone his torch over the sitting room. Father Christmas hadn't been. The room was exactly as he'd left it that evening.

Except for one thing. Henry's light illuminated the Christmas tree, heavy with chocolate santas and chocolate bells and chocolate reindeer. Mum and Dad must have hung them on the tree after he'd gone to bed.

Horrid Henry looked at the chocolates cluttering up the Christmas tree. Shame, thought Horrid Henry, the way those chocolates spoil the view of all those lovely decorations. You could barely see the baubles and tinsel he and Peter had worked so hard to put on.

'Hi, Henry,' said the chocolate santas. 'Don't you want to eat us?'

'Go on, Henry,' said the chocolate

bells. 'You know you want to.'

'What are you waiting for, Henry?' urged the chocolate reindeer.

What indeed? After all, it *was* Christmas.

Henry took a chocolate santa or three from the side, and then another two from the back. Hmmn, boy, was that great chocolate, he thought, stuffing them into his mouth.

Oops. Now the chocolate santas looked a little unbalanced.

Better take a few from the front and from the other side, to even it up, thought Henry. Then no one will notice there are a few chocolates missing.

Henry gobbled and gorged and guzzled. Wow, were those chocolates yummy!!!

The tree looks a bit bare, thought Henry a little while later. Mum had such eagle eyes she might notice that a few— well, all—of the chocolates were missing. He'd better hide all those gaps with a

few extra baubles. And, while he was
improving the tree, he could swap that
stupid fairy for Terminator Gladiator.

Henry piled extra decorations onto the
branches. Soon the Christmas tree was so
covered in baubles and tinsel there
was barely a hint of green. No one would
notice the missing chocolates. Then
Henry stood on a chair, dumped the
fairy, and, standing on his tippy-tippy
toes, hung Terminator Gladiator at the
top where he belonged.

Perfect, thought Horrid Henry, jumping off the chair and stepping back to admire his work. Absolutely perfect. Thanks to me this is the best tree ever.

There was a terrible creaking sound. Then another. Then suddenly . . .

CRASH!

114

The Christmas tree toppled over.

Horrid Henry's heart stopped.

Upstairs he could hear Mum and Dad
stirring.

'Oy! Who's down there?' shouted Dad.

RUN!!! thought Horrid Henry. Run
for your life!!

Horrid Henry ran like he had never run
before, up the stairs to his room before
Mum and Dad could catch him. Oh please
let him get there in time. His parents'

115

bedroom door opened just as Henry
dashed inside his room. He'd made it.
He was safe.

SPLASH! The bucket of water
spilled all over him.

TRIP! Horrid Henry fell over the
skipping rope.

CRASH! SMASH!
RING! RING! jangled the bells.
PLLLLLLL!
belched the whoopee cushions.

'What is going on in here?' shrieked Mum, glaring.

'Nothing,' said Horrid Henry, as he lay sprawled on the floor soaking wet and tangled up in threads and wires and rope. 'I heard a noise downstairs so I got up to check,' he added innocently.

'Tree's fallen over,' called Dad. 'Must have been overloaded. Don't worry, I'll sort it.'

'Get back to bed, Henry,' said Mum wearily. 'And don't touch your stocking till morning.'

Henry looked. And gasped. His stocking was stuffed and bulging. That mean old sneak, thought Horrid Henry indignantly. How did he do it? How had he escaped the traps?

Watch out Father Christmas, thought Horrid Henry. I'll get you next year.

117

DECEMBER 13TH

12
DAYS TILL
CHRISTMAS!

Why does Santa wear bright red braces?

To hold his trousers up.

DECEMBER 14ᵀᴴ

11
DAYS TILL
CHRISTMAS!

What did one angel say to the other?

Halo there.

DECEMBER 15TH

10

DAYS TILL CHRISTMAS!

What did the sheep say to the shepherd?

Season's bleatings.

HORRID HENRY'S CHRISTMAS

Perfect Peter sat on the sofa looking through the Toy Heaven catalogue. Henry had hogged it all morning to write his Christmas present list. Naturally, this was not a list of the presents Henry planned to give. This was a list of what he wanted to get.

Horrid Henry looked up from his work. He'd got a bit stuck after: a million pounds, a parrot, a machete, swimming pool, trampoline, and Killer Catapult.

'Gimme that!' shouted Horrid Henry. He snatched the Toy Heaven catalogue from Perfect Peter.

'You give that back!' shouted Peter.

'It's my turn!' shouted Henry.

'You've had it the whole morning!' shrieked Peter. 'Mum!'

'Stop being horrid, Henry,' said Mum, running in from the kitchen.

Henry ignored her. His eyes were glued to the catalogue. He'd found it. The toy of his dreams. The toy he had to have.

'I want a Boom-Boom Basher,' said Henry. It was a brilliant toy which crashed into everything, an ear-piercing siren wailing all the while. Plus all the trasher attachments. Just the thing for knocking down Perfect Peter's marble run.

'I've got to have a Boom-Boom Basher,' said Henry, adding it to his list in big letters.

'Absolutely not, Henry,' said Mum. 'I will not have that horrible noisy toy in my house.'

'Aw, come on,' said Henry. 'Pleeease.'

Dad came in.

'I want a Boom-Boom Basher for Christmas,' said Henry.

'No way,' said Dad. 'Too expensive.'

'You are the meanest, most horrible parents in the whole world,' screamed Henry. 'I hate you! I want a Boom-Boom Basher!'

'That's no way to ask, Henry,' said Perfect Peter. 'I want doesn't get.'

Henry lunged at Peter. He was an octopus squeezing the life out of the helpless fish trapped in its tentacles.

'Help,' spluttered Peter.

'Stop being horrid, Henry, or I'll cancel the visit to Father Christmas,' shouted Mum.

Henry stopped.

The smell of burning mince pies drifted into the room.

'Ahh, my pies!' shrieked Mum.

★

'How much longer are we going to have to wait?' whined Henry. 'I'm sick of this!'

Horrid Henry, Perfect Peter, and Mum were standing near the end of a very long queue waiting to see Father Christmas. They had been waiting for a very long time.

'Oh, Henry, isn't this exciting,' said Peter. 'A chance to meet Father Christmas. I don't mind how long I wait.'

'Well I do,' snapped Henry. He began to squirm his way through the crowd.

'Hey, stop pushing!' shouted Dizzy Dave.

'Wait your turn!' shouted Moody Margaret.

'I was here first!' shouted Lazy Linda.

Henry shoved his way in beside Rude Ralph.

'What are you asking Father Christmas for?' said Henry. 'I want a Boom-Boom Basher.'

'Me too,' said Ralph. 'And a Goo-Shooter.'

Henry's ears pricked up.

'What's that?'

'It's really cool,' said Ralph. 'It splatters green goo over everything and everybody.'

'Yeah!' said Horrid Henry as Mum dragged him back to his former place in the queue.

★

'What do you want for Christmas, Graham?' asked Santa.

'Sweets!' said Greedy Graham.

'What do you want for Christmas, Bert?' asked Santa.

'I dunno,' said Beefy Bert.

'What do you want for Christmas, Peter?' asked Santa.

'A dictionary!' said Peter. 'Stamps, seeds, a geometry kit, and some cello music, please.'

'No toys?'

'No thank you,' said Peter. 'I have plenty of toys already. Here's a present for you, Santa,' he added, holding out a beautifully wrapped package. 'I made it myself.'

'What a delightful young man,' said Santa. Mum beamed proudly.

'My turn now,' said Henry, pushing Peter off Santa's lap.

'And what do you want for Christmas, Henry?' asked Santa.

Henry unrolled the list.

'I want a Boom-Boom Basher and a Goo-Shooter,' said Henry.

'Well, we'll see about that,' said Santa.

'Great!' said Henry. When grown-ups said 'We'll see,' that almost always meant 'Yes.'

It was Christmas Eve.

Mum and Dad were rushing around the house tidying up as fast as they could.

Perfect Peter was watching a nature programme on TV.

'I want to watch cartoons!' said Henry. He grabbed the clicker and switched channels.

'I was watching the nature programme!' said Peter. 'Mum!'

'Stop it, Henry,' muttered Dad. 'Now, both of you, help tidy up before your aunt and cousin arrive.'

Perfect Peter jumped up to help.

Horrid Henry didn't move.

'Do they have to come?' said Henry.

'Yes,' said Mum.

'I hate cousin Steve,' said Henry.

'No you don't,' said Mum.

'I do too,' snarled Henry. If there was a yuckier person walking the earth than Stuck-up Steve, Henry had yet to meet him. It was the one bad thing about Christmas, having him come to stay every year.

Ding Dong. It must be Rich Aunt Ruby and his horrible cousin. Henry watched as his aunt staggered in carrying boxes and boxes of presents which she dropped under the brightly-lit tree. Most of them, no doubt, for Stuck-up Steve.

'I wish we weren't here,' moaned
Stuck-up Steve. 'Our house is so much
nicer.'

'Shh,' said Rich Aunt Ruby. She went
off with Henry's parents.

Stuck-up Steve looked down at
Henry.

'Bet I'll get loads more presents than you,' he said.

'Bet you won't,' said Henry, trying to sound convinced.

'It's not what you get it's the thought that counts,' said Perfect Peter.

'*I'm* getting a Boom-Boom Basher *and* a Goo-Shooter,' said Stuck-up Steve.

'So am I,' said Henry.

'Nah,' said Steve. 'You'll just get horrible presents like socks and stuff. And won't I laugh.'

When I'm king, thought Henry, I'll have a snake pit made just for Steve.

'I'm richer than you,' boasted Steve. 'And I've got loads more toys.' He looked at the Christmas tree.

'Call that twig a tree?' sneered Steve. 'Ours is so big it touches the ceiling.'

'Bedtime, boys,' called Dad. 'And remember, no one is to open any presents until we've eaten lunch and gone for a walk.'

'Good idea, Dad,' said Perfect Peter. 'It's always nice to have some fresh air on Christmas Day and leave the presents for later.'

Ha, thought Horrid Henry. We'll see about that.

The house was dark. The only noise was the rasping sound of Stuck-up Steve, snoring away in his sleeping bag.

Horrid Henry could not sleep. Was

there a Boom-Boom Basher waiting for
him downstairs?

He rolled over on his side and tried
to get comfortable. It was no use. How
could he live until Christmas morning?

Horrid Henry could bear it no longer.
He had to find out if he'd been given a
Boom-Boom Basher.

Henry crept out of bed, grabbed
his torch, stepped over Stuck-up Steve –
resisting the urge to stomp on him – and
sneaked down the stairs.

136

CR-EEAK went the creaky stair. Henry froze.

The house was silent.

Henry tiptoed into the dark sitting room. There was the tree. And there were all the presents, loads and loads and loads of them!

Right, thought Henry, I'll just have a quick look for my Boom-Boom Basher and then get straight back to bed.

He seized a giant package. This looked promising. He gave it a shake. Thud-thud-thunk. This sounds good, thought Henry. His heart leapt. I just know it's a Boom-Boom Basher. Then he checked the label: 'Merry Christmas, Steve.'

Rats, thought Henry.

He shook another temptingly-shaped present: 'Merry Christmas, Steve.' And another: 'Merry Christmas, Steve.' And another. And another.

Then Henry felt a small, soft, squishy

package. Socks for sure. I hope it's not for me, he thought. He checked the label: 'Merry Christmas, Henry.'

There must be some mistake, thought Henry. Steve needs socks more than I do. In fact, I'd be doing him a favour giving them to him.

Switch! It was the work of a moment to swap labels.

Now, let's see, thought Henry. He eyed a Goo-Shooter shaped package with Steve's name on it, then found another, definitely book-shaped one, intended for himself.

Switch!

Come to think of it, Steve had far too many toys cluttering up his house. Henry had heard Aunt Ruby complaining about the mess just tonight.

Switch! Switch! Switch! Then Horrid Henry crept back to bed.

It was 6:00 a.m.

'Merry Christmas!' shouted Henry. 'Time to open the presents!'

Before anyone could stop him Henry thundered downstairs.

Stuck-up Steve jumped up and followed him.

139

'Wait!' shouted Mum.

'Wait!' shouted Dad.

The boys dashed into the sitting room and flung themselves upon the presents. The room was filled with shrieks of delight and howls of dismay as they tore off the wrapping paper.

'Socks!' screamed Stuck-up Steve. 'What a crummy present! Thanks for nothing!'

'Don't be so rude, Steve,' said Rich Aunt Ruby, yawning.

'A Goo-Shooter!' shouted Horrid Henry. 'Wow! Just what I wanted!'

'A geometry set,' said Perfect Peter. 'Great!'

'A flower-growing kit?' howled Stuck-up Steve. 'Phooey!'

'Make Your Own Fireworks!' beamed Henry. 'Wow!'

'Tangerines!' screamed Stuck-up Steve. 'This is the worst Christmas ever!'

'A Boom-Boom Basher!' beamed
Henry. 'Gee, thanks. Just what I wanted!'

'Let me see that label,' snarled Steve.
He grabbed the torn wrapping paper.
'Merry Christmas, Henry,' read the label.
There was no mistake.

'Where's *my* Boom-Boom Basher?'

screamed Steve.

'It must be here somewhere,' said Aunt Ruby.

'Ruby, you shouldn't have bought one for Henry,' said Mum, frowning.

'I didn't,' said Ruby.

Mum looked at Dad.

'Nor me,' said Dad.

'Nor me,' said Mum.

'Father Christmas gave it to me,' said Horrid Henry. 'I asked him to and he did.'

Silence.

'He's got my presents!' screamed Steve. 'I want them back!'

'They're mine!' screamed Henry, clutching his booty. 'Father Christmas gave them to me.'

'No, mine!' screamed Steve.

Aunt Ruby inspected the labels. Then she looked grimly at the two howling boys.

'Perhaps I made a mistake when I labelled some of the presents,' she muttered to Mum. 'Never mind. We'll sort it out later,' she said to Steve.

'It's not fair!' howled Steve.

'Why don't you try on your new socks?' said Horrid Henry.

Stuck-up Steve lunged at Henry. But Henry was ready for him.

SPLAT!

'Aaaarggh!' screamed Steve, green goo

dripping from his face and clothes and
hair.

'HENRY!' screamed Mum and Dad.

'How could you be so horrid!'

'Boom-Boom CRASH! NEE NAW
NEE NAW WHOO WHOOO
WHOOO!'

What a great Christmas, thought Henry,

as his Boom–Boom Basher knocked over Peter's marble run.

'Say goodbye to Aunt Ruby, Henry,' said Mum. She looked tired.

Rich Aunt Ruby and Steve had decided to leave a little earlier than planned.

'Goodbye, Aunt,' said Henry. 'Goodbye, Steve. Can't wait to see you next Christmas.'

'Actually,' said Mum, 'you're staying the night next month.'

Uh-oh, thought Horrid Henry.

DECEMBER 16TH

9
DAYS TILL
CHRISTMAS!

What's the definition of a balanced diet?

A Christmas cake in each hand.

DECEMBER 17ᵀᴴ

8

DAYS TILL
CHRISTMAS!

What Christmas carol do Horrid Henry's parents like?

Silent night.

DECEMBER 18TH

7

DAYS TILL
CHRISTMAS!

(JUST I WEEK TO GO!

What does Santa do when his elves are naughty?

He gives them the sack.

HORRID HENRY'S CHRISTMAS LUNCH

'Oh, handkerchiefs, just what I wanted,' said Perfect Peter. 'Thank you *so* much.'

'Not handkerchiefs *again*,' moaned Horrid Henry, throwing the hankies aside and ripping the paper off the next present in his pile.

'Don't tear the wrapping paper!' squeaked Perfect Peter.

Horrid Henry ripped open the present and groaned.

Yuck (a pen, pencil, and ruler). Yuck
(a dictionary). Yuck (gloves). OK (£15—
should have been a lot more). Eeew (a
pink bow tie from Aunt Ruby). Eeew
(mints). Yum (huge tin of chocolates).
Good (five more knights for his army).
Very good (a subscription to Gross-Out
Fan Club) . . .

And (very very good) a Terminator
Gladiator trident . . . and . . .

And . . . where was the rest?

'Is that it?' shrieked Henry.

'You haven't opened my present,
Henry,' said Peter. 'I hope you like it.'

Horrid Henry tore off the wrapping. It
was a Manners With Maggie calendar.

'Ugh, gross,' said Henry. 'No thank
you.'

'Henry!' said Mum. 'That's no way to
receive a present.'

'I don't care,' moaned Horrid Henry.
'Where's my Zapatron Hip-Hop

dinosaur? And where's the rest of the
Terminator Gladiator fighting kit? I
wanted everything, not just the trident.'

'Maybe next year,' said Mum.

'But I want it now!' howled Henry.

'Henry, you know that "I want doesn't
get",' said Peter. 'Isn't that right, Mum?'

'It certainly is,' said Mum. 'And I
haven't heard you say thank you, Henry.'

Horrid Henry glared at Peter and
sprang. He was a hornet stinging a worm
to death.

'WAAAAAAH!' wailed Peter.

'Henry! Stop it or—'

Ding! Dong!

'They're here!' shouted Horrid Henry, leaping up and abandoning his prey. 'That means more presents!'

'Wait, Henry,' said Mum.

But too late. Henry raced to the door and flung it open.

There stood Granny and Grandpa, Prissy Polly, Pimply Paul, and Vomiting Vera.

'Gimme my presents!' he shrieked, snatching a bag of brightly wrapped gifts out of Granny's hand and spilling them on the floor. Now, where were the ones with his name on?

'Merry Christmas, everyone,' said Mum brightly. 'Henry, don't be rude.'

'I'm not being rude,' said Henry. 'I just

want my presents. Great, money!' said
Henry, beaming. 'Thanks, Granny! But
couldn't you add a few pounds and—'

'Henry, don't be horrid!' snapped Dad.

'Let the guests take off their coats,' said
Mum.

'Bleeeeech,' said Vomiting Vera,
throwing up on Paul.

'Eeeeek,' said Polly.

All the grown-ups gathered in the sitting
room to open their gifts.

'Peter, thank you so much for the
perfume, it's my favourite,' said Granny.

'I know,' said Peter.

'And what a lovely comic,
Henry,' said Granny.
'Mutant Max is my . . .
um . . . favourite.'

'Thank you,
Henry,' said
Grandpa. 'This
comic looks very
. . . interesting.'

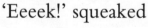

'I'll have it back
when you've
finished with it,' said Henry.

'Henry!' said Mum, glaring.

For some reason Polly didn't look
delighted with her present.

'Eeeek!' squeaked
Polly. 'This soap
has . . . hairs in
it.' She pulled
out a long
black one.

'That came

158

free,' said Horrid Henry.

'We're getting you toothpaste next year, you little brat,' muttered Pimply Paul under his breath.

Honestly, there was no pleasing some people, thought Horrid Henry indignantly. He'd given Paul a great bar of soap, and he didn't seem thrilled. So much for it's the thought that counts.

'A poem,' said Mum. 'Henry, how lovely.'

'Read it out loud,' said Grandpa.

'Dear old wrinkly Mum
Don't be glum
'Cause you've got a fat tum
And an even bigger...'

'Maybe later,' said Mum.

'Another poem,' said Dad. 'Great!'

'Let's hear it,' said Granny.

'Dear old baldy Dad—

. . . and so forth,' said Dad, folding Henry's poem quickly.

'Oh,' said Polly, staring at the crystal frog vase Mum and Dad had given her.

'How funny. This looks just like the vase *I* gave Aunt Ruby for Christmas last year.'

'What a coincidence,' said Mum, blushing bright red.

'Great minds think alike,' said Dad quickly.

Dad gave Mum an iron.

'Oh, an iron, just what
I always wanted,'
said Mum.

Mum gave Dad
oven gloves.

'Oh, oven gloves,
just what I always
wanted,' said Dad.

Pimply Paul gave
Prissy Polly a huge
power drill.

'Eeeek,' squealed
Polly. 'What's this?'

'Oh, that's the
Megawatt Superduper
Drill-o-matic 670
XM3,' said Paul, 'and just wait till you
see the attachments. You're getting those
for your birthday.'

'Oh,' said Polly.

Granny gave Grandpa a
lovely mug to put his false
teeth in.

Grandpa
gave Granny
a shower cap and a
bumper pack of dusters.

'What super presents!' said Mum.

'Yes,' said Perfect Peter. 'I loved every
single one of my presents, especially the
satsumas and walnuts in my stocking.'

'I didn't,' said Horrid Henry.

'Henry, don't be horrid,' said Dad.
'Who'd like a mince pie?'

'Are they homemade or from the
shop?' asked Henry.

'Homemade of course,' said Dad.

'Gross,' said Henry.

'Ooh,' said Polly. 'No, Vera!' she squealed as Vera vomited all over the plate.

'Never mind,' said Mum tightly. 'There's more in the kitchen.'

Horrid Henry was bored. Horrid Henry was fed up. The presents had all been opened. His parents had made him go on a long, boring walk. Dad had confiscated his Terminator trident when he had speared Peter with it.

So, what now?

Grandpa was sitting in the armchair with his pipe, snoring, his tinsel crown slipping over his face.

Prissy Polly and Pimply Paul were squabbling over whose turn it was to change Vera's stinky nappy.

'Eeeek,' said Polly. 'I did it last.'

'I did,' said Paul.

'WAAAAAAAAA!' wailed Vomiting Vera.

Perfect Peter was watching Sammy the Snail slithering about on TV.

Horrid Henry snatched the clicker and switched channels.

'Hey, I was watching that!' protested Peter.

'Tough,' said Henry.

Let's see, what was on? 'Tra la la la . . .' Ick! Daffy and her Dancing Daisies.

'Wait! I want to watch!' wailed Peter.

Click. ' . . . and the tension builds as the judges compare tomatoes grown . . . ' Click! ' . . . wish you a Merry Christmas, we wish you . . .' Click! 'Chartres Cathedral is one of the wonders of . . . ' Click! 'HA HA HA HA HA HA HA HA.' Opera! Click! Why was there nothing good on TV?

Just a baby movie about singing cars he'd seen a million times already.

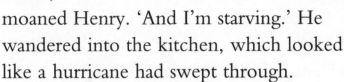

'I'm bored,' moaned Henry. 'And I'm starving.' He wandered into the kitchen, which looked like a hurricane had swept through.

'When's lunch? I thought we were eating at two. I'm starving.'

'Soon,' said Mum. She looked a little

frazzled. 'There's been a little problem with the oven.'

'So when's lunch?' bellowed Horrid Henry.

'When it's ready!' bellowed Dad.

Henry waited. And waited. And waited.

'When's lunch?' asked Polly.

'When's lunch?' asked Paul.

'When's lunch?' asked Peter.

'As soon as the turkey is cooked,' said Dad. He peeked into the oven. He poked the turkey. Then he went pale.

'It's hardly cooked,' he whispered.

'Check the temperature,' said Granny.

Dad checked.

'Oops,' said Dad.

'Never mind, we can start with the sprouts,' said Mum cheerfully.

'That's not the right way to do sprouts,' said Granny. 'You're peeling too many of the leaves off.'

'Yes, Mother,' said Dad.

'That's not the right way to make bread sauce,' said Granny.

'Yes, Mother,' said Dad.

'That's not the right way to make stuffing,' said Granny.

'Yes, Mother,' said Dad.

'That's not the right way to roast potatoes,' said Granny.

'Mother!' yelped Dad. 'Leave me alone!'

'Don't be horrid,' said Granny.

'I'm not being horrid,' said Dad.

'Come along Granny, let's get you a nice drink and leave the chef on his own,' said Mum, steering Granny firmly towards the sitting room. Then she stopped.

'Is something burning?' asked Mum, sniffing.

Dad checked the oven.

'Not in here.'

There was a shriek from the sitting room.

'It's Grandpa!' shouted Perfect Peter.

Everyone ran in.

There was Grandpa, asleep in his chair. A thin column of black smoke rose from

the arms. His paper crown, drooping
over his pipe, was smoking.

'Whh..whh?' mumbled Grandpa, as
Mum whacked him with her broom.
'AAARRGH!' he gurgled as Dad threw
water over him.

'When's lunch?' screamed Horrid
Henry.

'When it's ready,' screamed Dad.

★

It was dark when Henry's family finally sat down to Christmas lunch. Henry's tummy was rumbling so loudly with hunger he thought the walls would cave in. Henry and Peter made a dash to grab the seat against the wall, furthest from the kitchen.

'Get off!' shouted Henry.

'It's my turn to sit here,' wailed Peter.

'Mine!'

'Mine!'

Slap!

Slap!

'WAAAAAAAAAAA!' screeched Henry.

'WAAAAAAAAAAAA!' wailed Peter.

'Quiet!' screamed Dad.

Mum brought in fresh holly and ivy to decorate the table.

'Lovely,' said Mum, placing the boughs all along the centre.

'Very festive,' said Granny.

'I'm starving!' wailed Horrid Henry.

'This isn't Christmas lunch, it's Christmas dinner.'

'Shhh,' said Grandpa.

The turkey was finally cooked. There were platefuls of stuffing, sprouts, cranberries, bread sauce and peas.

'Smells good,' said Granny.

'Hmmn, boy,' said Grandpa. 'What a feast.'

Horrid Henry was so hungry he could eat the tablecloth.

'Come on, let's eat!' he said.

'Hold on, I'll just get the roast potatoes,' said Dad. Wearing his new oven gloves, he carried in the steaming hot potatoes in a glass roasting dish, and set it in the middle of the table.

'*Voila*!' said Dad. 'Now, who wants dark meat and who . . .'

'What's that crawling . . . aaaarrrghh!' screamed Polly. 'There are spiders every-where!'

Millions of tiny spiders were pouring from the holly and crawling all over the table and the food.

'Don't panic!' shouted Pimply Paul, leaping from his chair, 'I know what to do, we just—'

But before he could do anything the glass dish with the roast potatoes exploded.

CRASH!

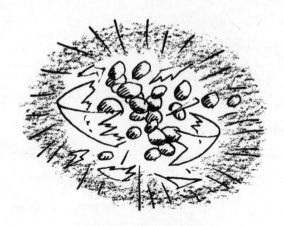

SMASH!

'EEEEEKK!' screamed Polly.

Everyone stared at the slivers of glass glistening all over the table and the food.

Dad sank down in his chair and covered his eyes.

'Where are we going to get more food?' whispered Mum.

'I don't know,' muttered Dad.

'I know,' said Horrid Henry, 'let's start with Christmas pudding and defrost some pizzas.'

Dad opened his eyes.

Mum opened her eyes.

'That,' said Dad, 'is a brilliant idea.'

'I really fancy some pizza,' said Grandpa.

'Me too,' said Granny.

Henry beamed. It wasn't often his ideas were recognised for their brilliance.

'Merry Christmas everyone,' said Horrid Henry. 'Merry Christmas.'

DECEMBER 19th

6
DAYS TILL
CHRISTMAS!

How does Rudolph know when Christmas is coming?

He looks at his calen-deer.

Why are Christmas trees like bad knitters?

They both drop their needles!

DECEMBER 21ˢᵀ

4
DAYS TILL
CHRISTMAS!

Who delivers the cat's Christmas presents?

Santa Paws.

HOW TO SURVIVE...
CHRISTMAS CHAOS WITH
HORRID HENRY

Christmas! Presents! Presents! Presents! Chocolate! Presents! More chocolate! Presents! All day telly! Presents!

That, of course, is how Christmas should be. No pesky relatives clogging up the sofa and hogging the telly, no horrible little brothers, and no sprouts EVER.
With my fool-proof, 100% tried and tested survival guide, you can have the Christmas YOU deserve, this year, and the next and the next...
No more bad presents. All the chocolate you want. Little brothers and sisters firmly in their box where they belong.

So what are you waiting for? Stop reading this and get plotting!

Henry

HORRID HENRY'S TOP CHRISTMAS MOTTOS

☆ Getting is better than giving.

☆ Save up your pocket money – then spend it on yourself.

☆ Worms don't get presents.

☆ Beware the wrinklies – currants, raisins and grandparents.

☆ Sprouts make you bald.

☆ Every present you buy means something you can't buy for yourself.

☆ I want … gets.

☆ Satsumas are NOT presents.

HORRID HENRY'S CRAFTY ADVENT CALENDAR

You will need

a large piece of stiff card
pencils, paints and felt tip pens
sticky tape
silver foil or coloured tissue paper
scissors
24 sweets or chocolates

Instructions

1. Draw a Christmas tree on a piece of card-board and paint it green.
2. Wrap up sweets or chocolates in silver foil or coloured tissue paper.
3. Fasten the sweets to your Christmas tree picture with sticky tape.
4. Number the sweets 1 to 24 in any order, then enjoy a sweet every day until Christmas!

HENRY'S TIP: Remember, a big calendar means big sweets too!

CARDS TO RICH AUNT RUBY

Mum has written a letter to Aunt Ruby,
but Henry swaps it with a letter of his own.

Dear Ruby
We're all so looking forward to
having you and Steve for
Christmas this year. And
don't worry, Henry is delighted
to share his bedroom. I'm sure
the cousins will have loads of
fun together.
See you soon!
Love from your younger sister.

Dear Ruby

Sorry, no room here for you and Steve this Christmas. But drop off all your presents for Henry as soon as possible – no need to come in, just ring the bell and leave them at the door. He'd really like loads and loads and loads of cash. In fact, think of a huge sum, and then double it, to make up for the horrible lime green cardigan you gave him last year. And since there's no need to give Peter any presents, you can add his Christmas money to Henry's. Remember, Ruby, Christmas is all about giving so now's your chance to give give give to Henry

See you at Steve's next prison visit.

Your younger Sister

CONFUSED CHRISTMAS CARDS

Horrid Henry is the school Christmas postman. Can he deliver the right cards to the right people? Untangle the muddled-up names on each of the envelopes below.

1. GMAETARR

_ _ _ _ _ _ _ _

2. AILWMIL

_ _ _ _ _ _ _

3. PRHAL

_ _ _ _ _

4. RSM DBODOD

_ _ _ _ _ _ _

5. RREIUDGN

_ _ _ _ _ _ _ _

6. TBRE

_ _ _ _

CHRISTMAS CODE MESSAGE

Horrid Henry sends Ralph a secret code message in his Christmas card. Can you uncode Henry's message using the grid below?

	To Ralph Have a stinky Christmas Henry
D2/A5/A5/A1 D2/A5	__ __ __ __ __ __
B2/A1 A1/C3/A5	__ __ __ __ __
D5/A2/A3/D5/D1/A5	__ __ __ __ __ __
C3/B2/D3/B5	__ __ __ __
C1/D4/A3/A1	__ __ __ __
B2/A1	__ __
D3/D4/D4/D3!	__ __ __ __!

	1	2	3	4	5
A	T	U	R	K	E
B	Y	A	B	C	D
C	F	G	H	I	J
D	L	M	N	O	P
E	G	S	V	W	X

SURVIVING YOUR FAMILY AT CHRISTMAS

Pretend to be reading a book. Your parents will be so shocked they'll leave you alone. (Remember to hide a comic inside.)

Pretend to be deaf.

Hide in your
room with
your music
on full blast.

Do your chores so badly, and slowly, that
your parents won't bother you again.

END-OF-TERM SCHOOL SURVIVAL

Rehearsals had been going on forever. Horrid Henry spent most of his time slumping in a chair. He'd never seen such a boring play. Naturally he'd done everything he could to improve it.

'Can't I add a dance?' asked Henry.

'No,' snapped Miss Battle-Axe.

'Can't I add a teeny-weeny-little song?' Henry pleaded.

'No!' said Miss Battle-Axe.

'But how does the innkeeper *know* there's no room?' said Henry. 'I think I should—'

Miss Battle-Axe glared at him with her red eyes.

'One more word from you, Henry, and you'll change places with Linda,' snapped Miss Battle-Axe. 'Blades of grass, let's try again ...'

Does Henry survive the School Nativity? Find out in 'Horrid Henry's Christmas Play' from *Horrid Henry's Cracking Christmas*.

CHRISTMAS PLAY CRISS-CROSS

Fit all the parts of the School Christmas Play into the criss-cross puzzle.

4 letters
MARY
STAR

5 letters
SHEEP
JESUS
GRASS
ANGEL

6 letters
JOSEPH
DONKEY

8 letters
SHEPHERD

9 letters
INNKEEPER

CLUE: Fit Horrid Henry's part into the puzzle first!

SURVIVING THE SCHOOL CHRISTMAS PLAY

When Miss Battle-Axe is giving out
the parts, shout very loudly –
'I WANT TO BE JOSEPH!'

Refuse to be a blade of grass –
it's the worst part.

Trick the leading actor into leaving the
show.
Then offer to replace him.

If all else fails – make your own
part BIGGER.

CLEVER CLARE'S CHRISTMAS QUIZ

1. Postmen in Victorian England were sometimes called 'robins' because:

   (a) Their uniforms were red
   (b) Their noses were red
   (c) Their hair was red

2. The little sausages wrapped in bacon that we eat at Christmas lunch are called:

(a) Sausages in bed
(b) Pigs in a blanket
(c) Pigs' trotters

3. The first sort of Christmas pudding was like porridge and it was called:

   (a) Frumenty
   (b) Glop
   (c) Ready Brek

4. When should you take down your Christmas decorations?

(a) Never – just leave your mum and dad to do it

(b) 24th December
(c) 6th January

5. Nowadays mince pies are filled with:

(a) Raisins and sultanas
(b) Minced beef
(c) Peanut butter and jelly

6. Why is Boxing Day so called?

(a) A big boxing match was always held on that day
(b) It was the day for sharing the Christmas Box with the poor
(c) Little brothers and sisters should be put into a box for the day

Check out the answers on page 258.
What's your score?

Clever Clare says:

0-2 You're clueless about Christmas! Just like Horrid Henry, I bet you think it's all about presents.

3-4 You're quite clued-up, but maybe your brain is ready for a long rest over the Christmas holidays.

5-6 Happy Christmas! You're almost as clever as me!

SANTA'S GROTTO

'What do you want for Christmas, Peter?' asked Santa.

'A dictionary!' said Peter. 'Stamps, seeds, a geometry kit, and some cello music, please.'

'No toys?'

'No thank you,' said Peter. 'I have plenty of toys already. Here's a present for you, Santa,' he added, holding out a beautifully wrapped package. 'I made it myself.'

'What a delightful young man,' said Santa. Mum beamed proudly.

'My turn now,' said Henry, pushing Peter off Santa's lap.

'And what do you want for Christmas, Henry?' asked Santa.

Henry unrolled the list.

'I want a Boom-Boom Basher and a Goo-Shooter,' said Henry.

'Well, we'll see about that,' said Santa.

'Great!' said Henry. When grown-ups said 'We'll see,' that almost always meant 'Yes'.

Does Henry get the present he asks for? Find out in 'Horrid Henry's Christmas' from *Horrid Henry's Cracking Christmas*.

PUZZLING PRESENTS

Solve the crossword clues and find out what Horrid Henry and his family got for Christmas.

Across

2. Pimply Paul gave Prissy Polly this Megawatt Superduper tool for making holes in walls.
4. Another present for Polly – it's for putting flowers in.
5. Horrid Henry wasn't pleased with this present which is used for writing thank you letters.
6. Dad gave this to Mum to keep his shirts wrinkle-free.

Down

1. See 3 down for this clue.
2. Grandpa gave Granny this present to get rid of all the dust in their house.
3. This clue is in two words – the first word fits in 3 down and the second fits in 1 down. Mum's present to Dad, used for holding hot things when he's cooking.

201

PERFECT PRESENTS...

Loads and loads of cash

Robomatic Supersonic
Space Howler Deluxe

Boom-Boom Basher

Day-Glo slime

Terminator Gladiator
Fighting Kit

Bugle Blast Boots

Zapatron Hip-Hop Dinosaur

Strum 'N' Drum

Huge tin of chocolates

...AND HOW TO GET THEM

Smile nicely at your parents and say 'pleeeeease'.

If that doesn't work, scream and shout 'I hate you!'

Write to Father Christmas and tell him to give you what you want this year.

Ambush Father Christmas and hold him hostage with a Goo-Shooter.

Dear Father Christmas
I want loads of money and a ROBOMATIC SUPERSONIC SPACE HOWLER with all the attachments
Mum and Dad want me to have one too.
Henry
P.S. Peter has been horrible all year and deserves NO presents
Please give his to me

GUESS THE PRESENT

Horrid Henry has a tag-swapping plan to avoid the presents he doesn't want. Help him guess what's inside by matching the parcels to the list of presents.

BOW TIE

GOO-SHOOTER

ZAPATRON HIP-HOP DINOSAUR

CELLO

TERMINATOR GLADIATOR TRIDENT

SOCKS

SATSUMA

DICTIONARY

CATAPULT

1.

2.

3.

4.

5.

6.

7.

8.

9.

205

WORST PRESENTS...

Lime-green cardigan

Pink frilly
lacy knickers

Socks

Satsumas

Dictionary

Baby Poopie
Pants Doll

...AND HOW NOT TO GET THEM

Sneak downstairs when everyone's asleep, and swap the present labels around.

Take the labels from your sock and Satsuma-shaped parcels and stick them on the Terminator Gladiator and Strum 'N' Drum-shaped ones instead.

Guess the shapes of the presents and hide the ones you don't want.

CHRISTMAS CLOCKWORDS

Horrid Henry swaps his most hated present for the chocolate bar in Perfect Peter's stocking. Follow the time instructions below to find out what it is.

Where does the big hand go when it's...

1. Half past five
2. Ten to six
3. Quarter past five
4. Twenty to six
5. Five past five
6. Twenty past five
7. Quarter to six

Answer: _ _ _ _ _ _ _

WHAT'S INSIDE?

Two parcels have arrived for Henry and Peter. Can you help Henry get the present he wants? In each of the boxes, cross out the letters that appear three times. Rearrange the remaining letters to find out what's inside.

L H x e L
a i O A
X i D A i
E h X E h

Answer: _ _ _ _

E R s y O
Y E O S
R s E O L
G y L r e

Answer: _ _ _

HOW TO SURVIVE THE THANK YOU LETTERS

Always tell your mum you'll write your thank you letters later…

…but if she says no TV till you've written them, try these sneaky tricks…

Make your handwriting as big as possible so it fills more space.

Write exactly the same letter to everybody.

Even better, write just one letter on the computer, like this:

Dear Sir or Madam

Thank you/no thank you for the
  a) wonderful
  b) horrible
  c) disgusting
present. I really loved/hated it. In fact it
is the best present/worst present I have ever
received. I played with it/broke it/ate it/spent
it/threw it in the bin straightaway.
Next time just send lots of money.

  Best wishes/worst wishes

                          Your friend or relative

THANK YOU LETTER

Henry writes Rich Aunt Ruby a thank you letter with pictures to puzzle her. Can you work out what he's written?

WHO SURVIVES THE CHRISTMAS CRUSH?

Horrid Henry, Rude Ralph and Moody
Margaret are determined to get Father
Christmas's last pot of
slime. Who survives
the Christmas crush
and wins?

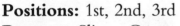

Positions: 1st, 2nd, 3rd
Presents: Slime, Crayons,
Sweets

	POSITION IN QUEUE	PRESENTS
HORRID HENRY		
MOODY MARGARET		
RUDE RALPH		

Clues

1. Moody Margaret gets pushed behind
   Rude Ralph in the queue.
2. Father Christmas gives the crayons
   to the 1st person in the queue.
3. Rude Ralph gets the sweets.

HOW TO AVOID SPENDING MONEY ON OTHER PEOPLE'S PRESENTS

Lend out your things as presents – you can take them back afterwards.

Make a sweet wrapper collage – you'll have to eat the sweets first!

Write poems for your
parents – when you're
a famous poet they'll
be proud to show off
your early work.

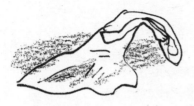

Find presents
around the house
– soap in the
bathroom, a cloth
from the kitchen,
or a very useful
plastic bag.

Give away
unwanted
presents from
last Christmas.

CHRISTMAS TREE TRIUMPHS

'Right, who wants
to decorate the tree?'
said Mum. She held
out a cardboard box brimming
with tinsel and gold and silver and blue baubles.

'Me!' said Henry.

'Me!' said Peter.

Horrid Henry dashed to the box and scooped up as
many shiny ornaments as he could.

'I want to put on the gold baubles,' said Henry.

'I want to put on the tinsel,' said Peter.

'Keep away from my side of the tree,' hissed Henry.

'You don't have a side,' said Peter.

'Do too.'

'Do not,' said Peter.

'I want to put on the tinsel *and* the baubles,'
said Henry.

'But I want to do the tinsel,' said Peter.

'Tough,' said Henry, draping Peter in tinsel.

'**Muuum!**' wailed Peter.

Find out if Henry gets his way in 'Horrid Henry's
Christmas Presents' from *Horrid Henry's Cracking Christmas*.

CHRISTMAS TREE WORDSEARCH

Can you find all the Christmas Tree words in the wordsearch?

FAIRY
TINSEL
BAUBLES
TREE
STAR
LIGHTS
BELLS
RIBBONS
BOWS
GARLAND
BERRIES
CONES

S	E	N	O	C	S	T	E	B
L	E	R	M	T	I	R	G	E
L	R	N	A	A	I	T	A	R
E	T	R	O	B	R	G	R	R
B	A	U	B	L	E	S	L	I
L	B	O	W	S	A	D	A	E
I	N	Y	R	I	A	F	N	S
S	T	I	N	S	E	L	D	A
T	O	R	S	T	H	G	I	L

The left-over letters reveal what Horrid Henry wants to put on the top of the Christmas tree:

_ _ _ _ _ _ _ _   _ _ _ _ _ _ _ _

SPOT THE
DIFFERENCE

1. _____

2. _____

3. _____

Can you spot the six differences between
the two pictures?

4. _____

5. _____

6. _____

HOW TO SNEAK THE CHOCOLATES OFF THE TREE

EITHER

Sneak down at night when everyone else is asleep.

OR

Offer to decorate the tree – and hide half the chocolates! You can sneak the rest later.

CHRISTMAS SUDOKU

All four squares, all four rows and all four columns must include one holly leaf, one bauble, one star and one candle. Can you solve it?

FATHER CHRISTMAS FUN

Horrid Henry lay on the sofa with his fingers in his ears, double-checking his choices from the Toy Heaven catalogue. Big red 'X's' appeared on every page, to help you-know-who remember all the toys he absolutely had to have. Oh please, let everything he wanted leap from its pages and into Santa's sack.

After all, what could be better than looking at a huge, glittering sack of presents on Christmas morning, and knowing that they were all for you?

Oh please let this be the year when he finally got everything he wanted!

Does Henry get everything he wants? Find out in 'Horrid Henry's Ambush' from *Horrid Henry's Cracking Christmas*.

HAVE YOU BEEN HORRID OR PERFECT THIS YEAR?

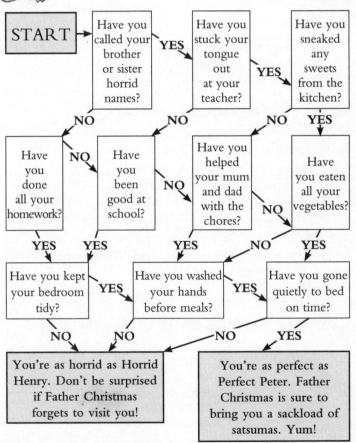

CRISS–CROSS CHRISTMAS JOKES

MARY	TOAD
PUDDLE	TROUSERS
SOOTS	TURKEY

1. Why does Father Christmas go down the chimney?

   Because it __ __ __ __ __ him.

2. Why does Santa wear bright red braces?

   To hold his __ __ __ __ __ __ __ __ up.

3. Who is never hungry at Christmas?

   The __ __ __ __ __ __ because he's always stuffed!

4. What is green, covered with tinsel and goes *ribbet ribbet*?

   Mistle- __ __ __ __ !

5. What do you call a snowman on a sunny day?

   A __ __ __ __ __ __ __

6. What is Father Christmas's wife called?

   __ __ __ __ Christmas.

Now fit the same six words into the criss-cross puzzle below.

CLUE: Start by fitting in the longest word.

225

CRAFTY CHRISTMAS STOCKINGS

These stockings are perfect for hanging on the tree and stuffing full of sweets and chocolates!

You will need

felt
scissors
craft glue

narrow ribbon
decorations – sequins, glitter or beads

Instructions

1. Cut two stocking shapes out of felt.

2. Carefully glue the two pieces together at the edges, leaving the top open.

3. Fold your ribbon in half to make a loop to hang on the tree. Glue inside the stocking.

4. Decorate your stocking with sequins, glitter or beads.

5. When the glue is dry, hang your stocking on the Christmas tree.

HORRID HENRY'S TIPS

**Don't mess about with a little stocking –
make a great big giant one.
Write a big message on your stocking
to Father Christmas, so he can't miss
it – FILL THIS WITH MONEY AND
CHOCOLATE. NO SATSUMAS OR
WALNUTS!**

Henry

SANTA'S REINDEER

Settle down and solve this puzzle while you're waiting for Father Christmas.

DASHER	C	H	U	V	T	G	P	O	R
DANCER	O	L	P	Y	I	R	U	E	A
PRANCER	M	Y	W	L	A	X	C	V	R
VIXEN	E	T	Q	N	O	N	E	M	E
COMET	T	D	C	Q	A	D	U	N	H
CUPID	T	E	J	D	I	P	U	C	S
DONNER	R	A	N	E	O	H	U	R	A
BLITZEN	D	O	N	N	E	R	R	Q	D
RUDOLPH	N	E	Z	T	I	L	B	R	U

SANTA'S MAZE

Help Henry find Santa's grotto in the shopping centre so he can make sure he gets everything on his list.

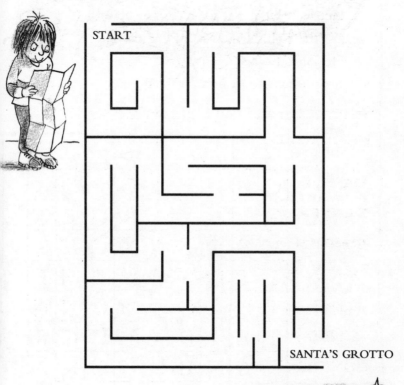

START

SANTA'S GROTTO

FESTIVE FOOD

It was dark when Henry's family finally sat down to Christmas lunch. Henry's tummy was rumbling so loudly with hunger he thought the walls would cave in. Henry and Peter made a dash to grab the seat against the wall, furthest from the kitchen.

'Get off!' shouted Henry.

'It's my turn to sit here,' wailed Peter.

'Mine!'

'Mine!'

Slap!

Slap!

'WAAAAAA AAAAAAAAA!' screeched Henry.

'WAAAAAA AAAAAAAAA!' wailed Peter.

'Quiet!' screamed Dad.

Find out whether Henry ever gets to eat in 'Horrid Henry's Christmas Lunch' from *Horrid Henry's Cracking Christmas*.

PUNCHLINE CROSS-OUT PUZZLE

Follow the instructions and find the punch-line to the joke. Fill in the left-over letters

Instructions

Cross out 4 Bs
Cross out 3 Fs
Cross out 5 Hs
Cross out 4 Js
Cross out 3 Ks
Cross out 4 Os
Cross out 3 Ts
Cross out 4 Xs

B	D	J	E	H	O	E
T	F	P	O	A	K	Z
N	B	H	D	J	C	B
K	R	F	O	I	T	C
S	K	P	J	X	A	H
H	N	D	O	E	T	F
V	B	J	E	H	X	N

How does good King Wenceslas like his pizzas?

_ _ _ _ _   _ _ _   _ _ _ _ _ _   _ _ _   _ _ _ _

HOW TO SURVIVE SPROUTS

Pickles
bread
potatoes
mincepies
pud
Choc biscuits
nuts
parsnips
sage and onion
onions
~~Sprouts~~
crisps

Cross 'sprouts' off Mum's shopping list and write 'crisps' instead.

Hide the bag of sprouts and throw it in the bin when Mum isn't looking.

Sneak the sprouts off your plate and into a drawer.

Save them for your Glop.

Flick them at Perfect Peter.

233

GRUESOME GLOP

Horrid Henry and Moody Margaret
love making Christmas Glop.

You will need

a big bowl
a wooden spoon
lots of yucky leftovers
from Christmas lunch

Instructions

1. Put the leftovers into the
   bowl and mix it all up
   into a gloppy Glop.
2. Invite your friends and
   family to a Glop tasting
   session. (Tee hee!)

**HORRID HENRY'S
GLOP SURPRISE**

Gravy
Brussel sprouts
Stuffing
Mashed Potato
Soup

**MOODY
MARGARET'S
SWEET AND SOUR**

White sauce
Cranberry sauce
Mincemeat
Christmas pudding
Lemonade

CHRISTMAS LUNCH CATASTROPHE

Find the words in the wordsearch. The first five left-over letters spell out Henry's ideal Christmas lunch.

S	S	P	B	I	Z	Y	Z	S	A
A	U	T	R	A	E	K	T	P	P
U	X	T	U	K	C	U	L	R	O
S	H	Y	R	F	N	O	G	O	T
A	K	U	F	T	F	R	N	U	A
G	T	Z	S	A	A	I	B	T	T
E	V	E	R	V	T	Z	N	S	O
S	H	J	Y	P	P	P	G	G	E
C	S	P	I	N	S	R	A	P	S
S	T	O	R	R	A	C	B	F	D

**TURKEY   CARROTS   SAUSAGES
STUFFING   PARSNIPS   CHESTNUTS
GRAVY   POTATOES
SPROUTS   BACON**

Henry's feast is: _ _ _ _ _

CHRISTMAS DAY DISASTERS

Ding Dong. It must be Rich Aunt Ruby and his horrible cousin. Henry watched as his aunt staggered in carrying boxes and boxes of presents which she dropped under the brightly-lit tree. Most of them, no doubt, for Stuck-up Steve.

'I wish we weren't here,' moaned Stuck-up Steve. 'Our house is so much nicer.'

'Shh,' said Rich Aunt Ruby. She went off with Henry's parents.

Stuck-up Steve looked down at Henry.

'Bet I'll get loads more presents than you,' he said.

'Bet you won't,' said Henry, trying to sound convinced.

'It's not what you get it's the thought that counts,' said Perfect Peter.

'*I'm* getting a Boom-Boom Basher *and* a Goo-Shooter,' said Stuck-up Steve.

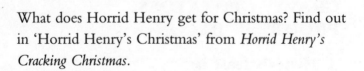

'So am I,' said Henry.

What does Horrid Henry get for Christmas? Find out in 'Horrid Henry's Christmas' from *Horrid Henry's Cracking Christmas*.

SPOT THE PAIRS

Mum gives Dad some flowery oven gloves for Christmas. Find the three matching pairs.

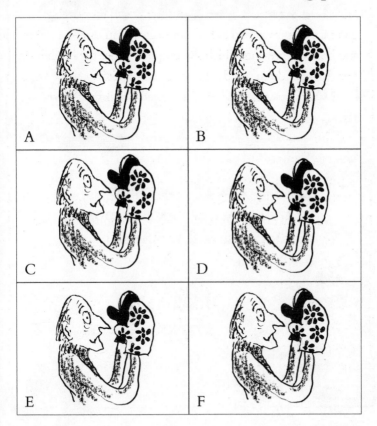

The three pairs are:

__ and __ , __ and __ , __ and __

DO THEY HAVE TO COME? SURVIVING THE RELATIVES

FOR

They give you presents.

They distract Mum and Dad so you can sneak more chocolates off the tree.

It's fun playing pranks on them!

They bring more chocolates!

AGAINST

You have to
give them
presents.

Sharing a bedroom with
Peter – blecccccch!

Having to be polite.

No TV!

CRAFTY CHRISTMAS CRACKERS

Crackers help Christmas to go with a bang!
Here's how to make your own.

You will need

2 loo rolls

strong glue

piece of crepe paper – big
enough to wrap around
your crackers

cracker 'bang' strip

cracker goodies

paper cut-outs to decorate

Instructions

1. Cut 1 loo roll in half.

2. Using the crepe paper, stick the three cardboard rolls along one side.

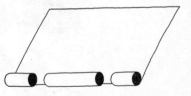

3. Holding the centre roll, carefully twist one of the end rolls.

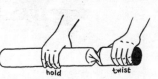

4. Insert the cracker 'bang' strip through the twisted end.

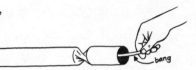

5. Fill the cracker with goodies, like sweets, stickers or a balloon and twist the other end of the tube to contain everything.

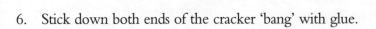

6. Stick down both ends of the cracker 'bang' with glue.

7. Decorate the cracker.

It's time to pull your cracker!

SURVIVING THE FAMILY GAMES

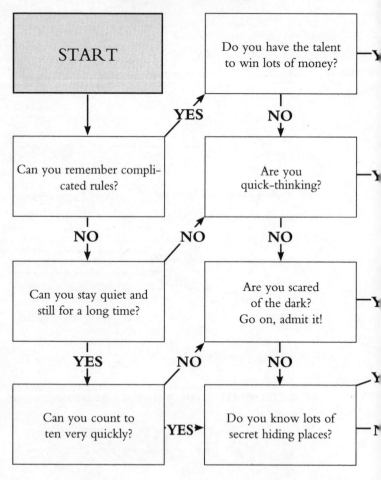

START

Do you have the talent to win lots of money? — Y

YES

Can you remember complicated rules?

NO

NO

Are you quick-thinking? — Y

NO

Can you stay quiet and still for a long time?

YES

NO

Are you scared of the dark? Go on, admit it! — Y

NO

Can you count to ten very quickly? — **YES**

Do you know lots of secret hiding places? — Y — N

Horrid Henry's top tip for surviving the family games – play a game you're sure to win.

| Can you cheat without anyone noticing? | **YES** → | Horrid Henry's favourite board game, GOTCHA, is just the game for a sneaky little money-grabber like you! |

NO ↓   **YES** ↗

| Are you brilliant at board games? | | With your acting talents and quick-thinking brain, you're sure to be a show-stopping champion at CHARADES. |

NO ↓   **YES** ↗

| Are you the best actor in your family? | | HIDE AND SEEK is the perfect game for someone as fast and fearless as you. |

NO ↓   **YES** ↗

| Are you faster on your feet than the rest of your family? | **NO** → | Whatever you play, you're going to lose! So turn on the TV and refuse to join in any silly family games. |

FIND THE PAIRS – CHRISTMAS TEAM GAM

You will need

20 old Christmas cards
scissors
two teams of players

How to play

1. Cut all the Christmas cards in half.
2. Put one batch of halves at one end of the room, and spread them out face-up on the floor.
3. Divide the remaining halves equally between the two teams.
4. Each team member in turn takes half a card, runs to the other end of the room, finds the matching piece and runs back to their team. The first team to complete all their ten cards is the winner.

HENRY'S HOW-TO-WIN TIP

When you divide out the cards, sneak the enemy team an extra card.

Henry

HENRY'S FAMILY CHRISTMAS QUIZ

Can you cope with one final challenge –
Horrid Henry's Family Christmas quiz?

1. HORRID HENRY asks: Where would I choose
to go for Christmas lunch?
(a) The Virtuous Veggie
(b) Gobble and Go
(c) Restaurant Le Posh

2. PERFECT PETER asks:
What starring role did I play
in the school Christmas play?
(a) Joseph
(b) A blade of grass
(c) The baby Jesus

3. MUM asks: What did I use to decorate
the table for Christmas lunch?
(a) Tinsel and baubles
(b) Fresh holly and ivy
(c) Satsumas and walnuts

4. DAD asks: If you bought me a CD for Christmas, what kind of music would I like best?

(a) Pop

(b) Heavy metal

(c) Classical

5. HORRID HENRY asks: What did I tell Father Christmas to give me?

(a) Loads and loads of cash

(b) A skipping rope

(c) Handkerchiefs

6. GRANNY asks: What did Perfect Peter give me for Christmas?

(a) A Mutant Max comic

(b) A skateboard

(c) My favourite perfume

7. PERFECT PETER asks: What did Henry want to put on the top of the Christmas tree?

(a) His teddy, Mr Kill

(b) Terminator Gladiator

(c) A fairy

8. PRISSY POLLY asks: What did Henry's mum and dad give me for Christmas?

(a) A crystal frog vase

(b) A power drill

(c) A pack of dusters

9. PIMPLY PAUL asks: What's the worst Christmas present I've ever received?

(a) A tube of pimple cream

(b) A big box of chocolates

(c) A piece of hairy soap

10. HORRID HENRY asks: In the school Christmas play, I played the innkeeper – what song did I sing?

(a) Silent Night

(b) Ten Green Bottles

(c) We Three Kings

Check out the answers on page 263. Did you do as well as Horrid Henry and his family? Henry gives his verdict:

1-4: Rubbish – this score's as sad as a soggy sprout!

5-7: Not bad – but not brilliant! Like Mum, Dad, Granny, Pimply Paul and Prissy Polly, you'll have to admit that you've been beaten by a better brain.

8-10: Congratulations! A cracking Christmas score. Peter just sneaked in with 8 – but the triumphant winner is ME with 10.

GOODBYE FROM HORRID HENRY

Goodbye, gang! Thanks to my
brilliant guide, I'm sure you'll
have the best Christmas
ever – tee hee!

DECEMBER 22ND

3
DAYS TILL
CHRISTMAS!

What did the big cracker say to the little cracker?

My pop is bigger
than yours.

DECEMBER 23RD

2
DAYS TILL
CHRISTMAS!

What's a gorilla's favourite Christmas song?

King Kong merrrily on high.

DECEMBER 24TH

1
DAY TILL
CHRISTMAS!

(IT'S CHRISTMAS EVE!)

How many chimneys does Father Christmas go down on Christmas Eve?

Stacks!

DECEMBER 25TH

IT'S CHRISTMAS DAY

HAPPY CHRISTMAS!

Who is never hungry at Christmas?

The turkey – he's always stuffed.

ANSWERS TO PUZZLES IN
HOW TO SURVIVE... CHRISTMAS CHAOS
WITH HORRID HENRY

page 190   Confused Christmas Cards

1. Margaret
2. William
3. Ralph
4. Mrs Oddbod
5. Gurinder
6. Bert

page 191   Christmas Code Message

MEET ME AT THE PURPLE HAND FORT AT NOON!

page 195   Christmas Play Criss-Cross

pages 198-199   Clever Clare's Christmas Quiz

1. (a)
2. (b)
3. (a)
4. (c)
5. (a)
6. (b)

page 201   Puzzling Presents

pages 204–205   Guess the Present

1. Goo-Shooter
2. Catapult
Trident
3. Zapatron Hip-Hop Dinosaur
4. Satsuma
5. Bow Tie

6. Socks
7. Terminator Gladiator

8. Dictionary
9. Cello

page 208   Christmas Clockwords

WALNUTS

page 209   What's Inside?

1. DOLL
2. GOO

page 212   Thank You Letter

Dear Aunt Ruby

I do not like my present. It's going in the bin.
Next Christmas, send me money. Send Peter a book. He's a worm.
Henry

	POSITION IN QUEUE	PRESENTS
HORRID HENRY	1st	CRAYONS
MOODY MARGARET	3rd	SLIME
RUDE RALPH	2nd	SWEETS

page 217   Christmas Tree Wordsearch

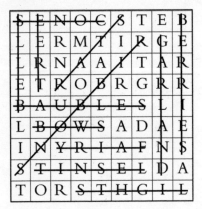

The hidden message is TERMINATOR GLADIATOR

pages 218-219   Spot the Difference

1. Henry has a piece of holly on his head.
2. The star is missing a point.
3. One of the baubles in the box is black.
4. One of the candles on the floor is missing.
5. There's an extra bauble on the tree.
6. The tree has a branch missing.

page 221 Christmas Sudoku

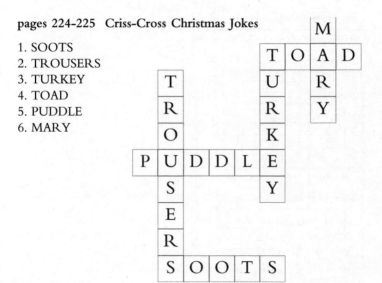

pages 224–225 Criss-Cross Christmas Jokes

1. SOOTS
2. TROUSERS
3. TURKEY
4. TOAD
5. PUDDLE
6. MARY

261

page 228 Santa's Reindeer

page 229 Santa's Maze

SANTA'S GROTTO

page 231 Punchline Cross-Out Puzzle

DEEP AND CRISP AND EVEN

262

page 235   Christmas Lunch Catastrophe

Henry's feast is: PIZZA

page 237   Spot the Pairs

The three pairs are:
A and E
B and C (one less petal on middle flower)
D and F (one petal more on top flower)

pages 245–247   Henry's Family Christmas Quiz

1. (b)
2. (a)
3. (b)
4. (c)
5. (a)
6. (c)
7. (b)
8. (a)
9. (c)
10. (b)

HORRID HENRY BOOKS

Storybooks

Horrid Henry
Horrid Henry and the Secret Club
Horrid Henry Tricks the Tooth Fairy
Horrid Henry's Nits
Horrid Henry Gets Rich Quick
Horrid Henry's Haunted House
Horrid Henry and the Mummy's Curse
Horrid Henry's Revenge
Horrid Henry and the Bogey Babysitter
Horrid Henry's Stinkbomb
Horrid Henry's Underpants
Horrid Henry Meets the Queen
Horrid Henry and the Mega-Mean Time Machine
Horrid Henry and the Football Fiend
Horrid Henry's Christmas Cracker
Horrid Henry and the Abominable Snowman
Horrid Henry Robs the Bank
Horrid Henry Wakes the Dead
Horrid Henry Rocks

Horrid Henry and the Zombie Vampire
Horrid Henry's Monster Movie
Horrid Henry's Nightmare
Horrid Henry's Guide to Perfect Parents
Horrid Henry's Krazy Ketchup
Horrid Henry's Cannibal Curse

Early Readers

Don't be Horrid Henry
Horrid Henry's Birthday Party
Horrid Henry's Holiday
Horrid Henry's Underpants
Horrid Henry Gets Rich Quick
Horrid Henry and the Football Fiend
Horrid Henry's Nits
Horrid Henry and Moody Margaret
Horrid Henry's Thank You Letter
Horrid Henry Car Journey
Moody Margaret's School
Horrid Henry's Tricks and Treats

Horrid Henry's Rainy Day
Horrid Henry's Author Visit
Horrid Henry Meets the Queen
Horrid Henry's Sports Day
Moody Margaret Casts a Spell
Horrid Henry's Christmas Presents
Moody Margaret's Makeover
Horrid Henry and the Demon Dinner Lady
Horrid Henry Tricks the Tooth Fairy
Horrid Henry's Homework
Horrid Henry and the Bogey Babysitter
Horrid Henry's Sleepover
Horrid Henry's Wedding
Horrid Henry's Haunted House
Horrid Henry's Mother's Day
Horrid Henry and the Comfy Black Chair
Horrid Henry and the Mummy's Curse
Horrid Henry and the Abominable Snowman

★

Colour books

Horrid Henry's Big Bad Book

Horrid Henry's Wicked Ways

Horrid Henry's Evil Enemies

Horrid Henry Rules the World

Horrid Henry's House of Horrors

Horrid Henry's Dreadful Deeds

Horrid Henry Shows Who's Boss

Horrid Henry's A-Z of Everything Horrid

Horrid Henry Fearsome Four

Horrid Henry's Royal Riot

Horrid Henry's Tricky Tricks

Joke Books

Horrid Henry's Joke Book

Horrid Henry's Jolly Joke Book

Horrid Henry's Mighty Joke Book

Horrid Henry versus Moody Margaret

Horrid Henry's Hilariously Horrid Joke Book

Horrid Henry's Purple Hand Gang Joke Book

Horrid Henry's All Time Favourite Joke Book
Horrid Henry's Jumbo Joke Book

★

Activity Books

Horrid Henry's Brainbusters
Horrid Henry's Headscratchers
Horrid Henry's Mindbenders
Horrid Henry's Colouring Book
Horrid Henry's Puzzle Book
Horrid Henry's Sticker Book
Horrid Henry Runs Riot
Horrid Henry's Annual 2015
Horrid Henry's Classroom Chaos
Horrid Henry's Holiday Havoc
Horrid Henry's Wicked Wordsearches
Horrid Henry's Mad Mazes
Horrid Henry's Crazy Crosswords

★

Fact Books

Horrid Henry's Ghosts
Horrid Henry's Dinosaurs
Horrid Henry's Sports
Horrid Henry's Food
Horrid Henry's King and Queens
Horrid Henry's Bugs
Horrid Henry's Animals
Horrid Henry's Ghosts
Horrid Henry's Crazy Creatures
Horrid Henry's World Records

★

Visit **Horrid Henry's** website at
www.horridhenry.co.uk for competitions,
games, downloads and a monthly newsletter

HORRID HENRY'S CANNIBAL CURSE

The final collection of four brand new utterly horrid stories in which Horrid Henry triumphantly reveals his guide to perfect parents, reads an interesting book about a really naughty girl, and conjures up the cannibal's curse to deal with his enemies and small, annoying brother.

HORRID HENRY'S KRAZY KETCHUP

Discover the one thing Horrid Henry is scared of, watch out for the return of Rabid Rebecca and find out what happens when Henry makes a film about his family.

HORRID HENRY'S MONSTER MOVIE

Henry makes his own scary movie, persuades
Peter to hand over his stash of Grump Cards,
spends a weekend at Aunt Ruby's with two of
his evilest arch-enemies, and sets up his own
Horrid Henry-style Olympics.

★